Critical acclaim for *You Are Not Alone*

"An extremely straightforward and honest account; I really enjoyed the read."

– **Shobhaa De,** Bestselling novelist and columnist

"A sensitive engaging story of the coming-of-age and finally finding love of a gay man in today's Mumbai"

– **Onir**, maker of acclaimed films, *My Brother Nikhil, Bas Ek Pal* and *Sorry Bhai*

"An enlightening, well-paced and provocative read, You Are Not Alone *challenges the everyday assumptions about close encounters of another kind and gives you enough reasons to read it"*

– **Dr. Akash Khurana**, actor and scriptwriter, in *The Queer Chronicle*

"A sensitive and absorbing account of a homosexual"

– **Randeep Wadehra**, *The Sunday Tribune*

"Beautifully written, it's a gay person's life in flashback"

– **Shobhna Kumar**, of queer-ink.com, in *Open* magazine

"Makes you nostalgic in bits and parts… it feels like you are peeping into someone's personal diary"

– **Priya**, gaysifamily.com

"Heart-wrenchingly beautiful; there is a bit of Sanjay in all of us, proving that 'we are not alone' in our thoughts and experiences.

– **Keith**, Editor, *The Queer Chronicle*

you are not alone

Arun Mirchandani

First published in India 2010 by **Frog Books**
an imprint of **Leadstart Publishing Pvt Ltd**
1 Level, Trade Centre
Bandra Kurla Complex
Bandra (East) Mumbai 400 051 India
Telephone: +91-22-40700804
Fax: +91-22-40700800
Email: info@leadstartcorp.com
www.leadstartcorp.com / www.frogbooks.net

Marketing Office:
Unit: 122 / Building B/2
First Floor, Near Wadala RTO
Wadala (East) Mumbai 400 037 India
Phone: +91-22-24046887

US Office:
Axis Corp, 7845 E Oakbrook Circle
Madison, WI 53717 USA

Copyright @ Arun Mirchandani

All rights reserved. No part of this publication may be reproduced, stored in or introduced into a retrieval system, or transmitted, in any form, or by any means (electronic, mechanical, photocopying, recording or otherwise) without the prior written permission of the publisher. Any person who does any unauthorised act in relation to this publication may be liable to criminal prosecution and civil claims for damages.

ISBN No: 978-93-80154-46-6

Publisher and Managing Editor: Sunil K Poolani
Editors: Arathi Menon & Vedika Burman
Design Editor: Mishta Roy

Typeset in Book Antiqua
Printed at Repro India Ltd, Mumbai

Price – India: Rs 195; Elsewhere: US $10

to
Ma

About the Author

Arun Mirchandani was born in 1982 in South Korea. He currently resides in Bombay, India. An alumnus from the Tata Institute of Social Sciences, Bombay, he is currently employed with a leading multinatinoal bank as part of their human resources team.

You Are Not Alone is Arun's first novel and he can be contacted at arunm28@yahoo.com

Prelude

Today I am 75 years old.

My name is Sanjay Sanghavi.

I lie here alone in my apartment staring at the ceiling. Suddenly, my whole life just whizzes before my eyes, I'm thinking back on the good times and the bad, I'm thinking of what my next life has in store for me, I'm waiting for the clock to stop ticking, I'm waiting for the pain to stop.

Prior to this, I had just walked out of my Pilates class, flirted a bit with my instructor, had a glass of juice over the reception counter chatting away with Suzette who just came home the previous night from her honeymoon (with her third husband) in Prague. I called for my chauffer (always hated the term driver) Ram, got into the plush backseat of my recently acquired BMW and told him to drive me home.

The security guard greets me with his usual warm smile, I smile back. The elevator doors open, and as soon as I enter, I notice I had spilled the juice on my designer track suit. Upset with myself about how stupid I could be to ruin, not any track suit but the one that cost me one third of my last drawn monthly salary, I pound on the door of my lavish 2,500-square-foot apartment instead of ringing the bell. Sunaina, my maid of many years opens the door and with the most sarcastic tone asks, "*Aaj Kya Hua?*" (What happened today?) She looks down at my pants and laughs, "*Arre sahab, yeh mein do minute mein gaayab kar doongi! Aap ke paas jaadugarni hain, kaay ki chinta?*" (Oh sahab, I'll get rid of this stain in two minutes! You have a magician with you, no worries!) I smile at her and move towards the couch. I sit down and switch on the television. The anchor on television is providing reviews on the recently released *The Curious Case of Benjamin Button*. She trashes the movie and I rubbish her review in my head. I smile and think to myself 'What a wonderful movie!'

Suddenly, I feel a shooting pain in my left arm, my chest hurts, I can't see anything.

I just had a heart attack. And while I sit there awaiting death, I look towards the wall in front of me cluttered with self portraits, photographs of loved ones and expensive pieces of art. Unexpectedly, the pain begins to slowly subside and my eyes start to force themselves shut. A few moments before closing my eyes, I catch a hazy glimpse of the picture of myself posing at the Bangalore Pride Parade and I smile.

CHAPTER 1

Today I am four years old.

Mom and dad wait anxiously outside the principal's office. Mom is quietly twiddling her thumbs and continuously chanting *Om Namah Shivay*. Dad on the other hand is pacing down the hallway similar to the time when my mom was in labour about to bear her first born, my older brother Rajiv. Mom looks towards dad, "Do you think he'll get through?" My dad walks up to mom, holds her hand and says "Rajiv made it three years ago, I'm sure Sanjay will make it to!"

Rajiv, my older brother was every parents dream child. He was a straight 'A' student, an athlete and a very diligent boy. When Rajiv interviewed to seek admission into Beverly American High, he was the only kid to have received a spot admission that year.

Beverly American High was one of the most sought after schools in Singapore and it was every NRI parent's goal to have their children admitted here. There was no second option of a school for an Indian parent in Singapore. If your kid didn't make it to Beverly American High, you would rather have him drop a year than admit him in any other school.

Mom and dad were not alone in their anxious wait. Also waiting outside the office were Mona and Harish Mehta - our closest family friends - to know the outcome of Sakhi's interview. Sakhi Mehta - my best friend. Last evening we were carefree, playing untroubled on the seesaw and this morning we smiled nervously at each other. While I waited at the holding area of the principal's office, Sakhi finished her round of interview. She smiled at me on her way out. She was asked to get her parents in. Sakhi was followed by aunty Mona and uncle Harish. Anxiety was written all over their faces, aunty Mona looked up praying to god one last time and uncle Harish wiped his brow with his handkerchief before entering the principal's cabin. I knew I was doomed as soon as I saw them step out of the cabin. I saw aunty Mona shedding tears of happiness and uncle Harish throwing Sakhi into the air in complete celebration. Sakhi was given a spot admission. A jubilant Sakhi gave me thumbs up on her way out wishing me luck for my interview.

"Sanjay Sanghavi!" called the pretty secretary, "It's your turn next!" She was curt and didn't even look in my direction while calling out my name. Come on, is it too much to ask for a warm smile before an interview? For Heavens' sake, I am four years old, I've never ever interviewed in my entire life till that day and the pressure of my best friend having received a spot admission was not helping at all.

I tried remembering all the instructions my mother gave me before I entered the room. "Knock on the door before you enter! Don't sit until you are asked to! Look at everybody in the room and say Good Morning! Don't speak until spoken to!" The list seemed exhaustive at the time and I'm pretty sure I remembered most of her advice.

I slowly knocked on the door and in the sweetest voice possible asked, "May I come in Sir?" The principal, Mr Cook smiled and said, pointing towards an empty chair "Of course, Son! Take a seat." I smiled, thanked him and again on my mother's instructions said, "Good morning Sir!" before I actually sat down. I could see he was pleased. The interview began. Solving the simple maths problems and answering the English grammar and logic related questions were cakewalk for me. I suddenly smelled success; I knew I would be given spot admission. I could envision my mom's happiness, dad's head held high up with pride and Rajiv's face green with envy. Well, of course I quickly snapped out of my day dreaming when the principal said, "We will now proceed to the last round of this selection process - Physical Activity!" "Physical Activity?" I thought to myself. I've never been good at physical activity. Till that point in my life, the only sport I had ever indulged in was arm wrestling with Rajiv (and I always lost). Mr Cook first asked me to walk the balance beam. One good look at the balance beam (which was a couple of meters long) and I knew that the moment I stepped on it, I would slip and fall. The last thing I wanted from this interview was a set of broken bones; the fear and anxiety of falling off the balance beam was so intense I felt tears rolling down my face. I looked at Mr Cook trying my best to hold back a howl and said "I can't!" With no sympathy reflecting on his face, Mr Cook looks down at his assessment sheet and scribbles something on it. He then points towards a soccer ball and says "Kick that ball into that goal!"

"This is easy," I thought to myself. Little did I know the moment I kicked the ball, it would roll over twice and stop. I'm sure that popular phrase used on the soccer field in the 80's "You kick like a girl!" was going to be replaced by "You kick like Sanjay Sanghavi!" I was so embarrassed by my attempt; I couldn't look up at Mr Cook. I continued staring at the end of the tie my mother had forced me to wear for the interview. I actually thought of making a dash for the exit and running for my life. But before I could act on my thought, Mr Cook says, "Do you know what the squats are?" Still gazing at the end of my tie, I nod my head in the affirmative. I had done the squats before as a punishment but never as a form of physical exercise.

"Give me 10!" he said. I move to the mat and after successfully squatting twice, I lose my balance on the third squat. I fall with my butt on the floor and legs in the air. "That will be all Mr Sanghavi!" I heard Mr Cook say. He called for his secretary, "Liz! Show Mr Sanghavi to the door and let his parents know." I knew this wasn't going to be good at all. Liz walked me to the door and with her curt tone in the direction of my parents said, "We'll let you know!" Thankfully the Mehta family had already left the premises by then (I didn't have to be subjected to public humiliation).

The ride back home was a long one. I kept thinking of how Sakhi was being treated to junk food somewhere to celebrate her success and I was only subjected to questioning and more questioning. "What happened? What kind of questions were you asked? Did you knock on the door before you entered? Did you greet the principal? Where do you think you goofed up?" Being the way I was, I chose not to answer any of their questions and pretended to be asleep. I knew I had not only goofed up, I was on my way to shatter the first dream my parents had for me.

Three days later I heard my mom scream on answering the door bell "It's here! It's here!" That was the letter from Beverly American High letting us know on whether I made it to the school or not. Mom placed the letter in front of the mini temple made in the house, prayed and then ripped the letter open. I was right there holding on to her *kurti* as anxious as she was. As soon as she read a few words from the letter, I saw a tear roll down her face.

She picked up the phone called dad and said, "Sanjay didn't make it! It says he isn't physically fit! We should wait another year! How could we? All of Sanjay's friends are going to be in school - Sakhi! Yogesh! Sachin! What do we do?" I could see none of my dad's reassurances on the other end of the phone were helping mom calm down. Mom was bawling like a baby and I could do nothing about it but blame myself. It was torturous to see my mother cry like that. I knew I had failed my parents and it was unfortunately not the first or the last time I did actually fail them.

Dad came home that evening, furious, handed me his briefcase and stormed into the bedroom where mom was sitting. He locked the door behind him. I quietly went to my bedroom, Rajiv was already fast asleep. I tried sleeping but couldn't. I kept wondering, 'Would I go to school that year? Will I miss a year? Will dad try admitting me in another school?'

Exactly a week later, Dad came home with a box of sweets and hugged mom as soon as he entered. "Sanjay made it to Beverly!" My mom with complete puzzlement managed to ask "How?" "I went to the school today and told them we hadn't heard from them." Mom was still puzzled "But we did hear from them..."

"I know that! And you know that! But they didn't know that! I blamed it on the postal services here. I threw the sympathy card, I told them that we have to have Sanjay admitted because his older brother Rajiv is already in the same school plus we haven't applied to any other school. This would mean Sanjay would have to miss out a complete year for no fault of his own but rather because of a mistake committed by the stupid postal department."

My mom grew more curious, "Then? Then what happened?" Dad continued, "They spoke to Mr Cook and they finally agreed to have Sanjay admitted on the condition that he would have to register for after school gymnasium practice. I agreed!" Mom and dad hugged again. Mom said, "Mona kept asking what the status on Sanjay's admission was. I didn't know what to say. She kept insisting that we go together for Sakhi and Sanjay's first day at school shopping. Now I will finally have something to say." Dad looked towards me and said "Have your bags packed son; you're going to Beverly American High!" I beamed with delight and went back to playing with my Barbie dolls.

******

It was four weeks before school actually started. Mom thought it would be a good idea to take Rajiv and me back home to Bombay for a few weeks. Mom wanted to visit *Nani* (grand-mom) and also thought this would be a well-deserved break for Rajiv who was being promoted to the third grade as an honor roll student. (An honor roll student was considered high potential and would be under observation the next academic year).

Finally the day I was looking forward to most in Bombay was here. Mom was to take us pre-school shopping that day. I almost went berserk in my head trying to make a list of what I wanted to buy - clothes! school bag! stationery! My poor mom did not know what she was in for. This was going to be one of the many embarrassing moments in her life, more embarrassing than the time I threw a tantrum asking her to buy me a Barbie doll in one of Singapore's hippest malls or the time I pulled my pants down in the middle of the amusement park just because I felt like.

We reached the entrance of a modest looking store called *Rustam Ki Dukaan*. As soon as I entered I was mesmerised by the colours in the store. Orange, Red, Purple, Yellow! With Rajiv in tow mom began browsing through the section for boy's clothes. Rajiv was picking out shirts, tee shirts, shorts for himself. Mom suddenly realised I was missing. She turned around and saw me staring at the bright colours that fascinated me so much. Mom called out to me "Sanjay! Sanjay! What are you doing there? Come here!"

I paid no heed and continued looking. Mom pulled me to the counter she was at and said "Here! Try this on!" With my gaze still on the striking shades, Mom forcibly got me to remove the tee I was wearing and try on the new shirt she was planning to buy for me. "Now, doesn't my Sanjay look like he is ready to charm his new friends at school? Look at yourself in the mirror! What do you think?"

Without looking at the mirror, I nodded in agreement and continued staring in the direction as earlier. I finally pointed out to a yellow *ghagra choli* (a traditional Indian dress for women) and said "I want that one!" Mom in a stern tone said, "Sanjay! You're a boy! That's for little girls! Now, do you want to be a girl?"

The tone of my voice got whinier and louder: "I WANT THAT ONE!"

"No you are not getting that one! You're never going to wear it!"

"I said I WANT THAT ONE! And I'm not leaving without it!"

"Sanjay! Behave yourself!"

I could hear Rajiv snickering and laughing, "Sanjay wants to be a girl! Sanjay wants to be a girl!" That did not make a difference to me at all. I stomped my feet and began wailing loudly. "I want that *ghagra choli*! I want that pretty yellow *ghagra choli*!"

I began gathering a lot of attention. In my head I knew my mission was being accomplished. One of the other women in the store walked up to my mom and said, "*Behehnji, apne bete ko laa do jo maang raha hain! Dress hi tho hain!*" (Sister, get your son what he wants. It is just a dress after all.)

Mom walked and asked the man across the counter how much the dress cost. The salesman thought since it's rare that he gets to see a queer boy like me walk into the store so he would have a little more fun at my family's expense. "*Madam, bete ko try nahin karni?*" (Madam, won't your son want to try the outfit?) "I want to try it! I want to try it!" I yelled.

Mom walked into the changing room with me and helped me try on the outfit. As soon as I tried it on, I ran out of the changing room to my brother Rajiv, I did a twirl and said, "Pretty, huh?" Rajiv looked at me in amazement while mom stood next to the changing room door holding back tears while everybody else in the store looked at her son and snickered. Mom wiped the tears from her face thinking if her son was really queer or if this was just a phase?

Today I am eight years old.

I could hear the clock ticking. I was awakened by something but didn't know exactly what. I looked out for the time; it was way past 1 am for sure. I had an early day at school tomorrow and tried to get myself back to sleep. But I couldn't.

I suddenly realised what was happening. I couldn't breathe. I was gasping. I tried to breathe through my mouth, but it wasn't helping. I wake up Rajiv. I was in no position to say anything so I pointed to my throat with heavy sighs indicating to Rajiv that something was wrong with me and that I needed help. Rajiv woke up screaming at the top of his lungs, pounding on the door of my parent's bedroom "MOM! DAD! Something's wrong with Sanjay! He can't breathe! He can't breathe!" Mom and dad rushed to my bedroom. Mom picked me up in her arms and instructed dad, "Call the hospital now! Ask them to send an ambulance! It is an asthma attack!" It was surprising how calm mom was at a time like this. I think all mothers have this special gift of knowing exactly what to do when their children fall ill. In her most soothing voice, she brushed my hair and said, "Sanjay, baby, everything is alright. It's only an asthma attack. Just stay awake and breathe through your mouth. The ambulance is going to be here any minute! And you're going to be just fine!" I believed my mom when she said that. It felt so reassuring; I stopped crying and began breathing through my mouth. I felt relieved.

After a couple of minutes, I heard the sound of the ambulance. I held mom's hand; she smiled reassuringly and accompanied me to the back of the ambulance. I held her hand so tight, I didn't want to let go. If I died at that moment, I was happy that at least I would die in my mother's arms. As soon as I reached the hospital, I was taken to the emergency room. As soon as I was taken in, mom howled. All her calmness disappeared. Rajiv cried at the sight of mom breaking down. Dad caught hold of her, hugged her tightly and said, "Relax honey! It's alright! Sanjay is stronger than that! He is and will always be a survivor!"

An hour and fifteen minutes later, Dr Hwang walked out of the emergency room, "Mr Sanghavi! Your son is doing fine; he is unconscious now because of the anesthesia, he should be awake in the morning, you can see him then."

"What went wrong?" Dad asked. "It was an asthma attack. Sanjay needs to be in the hospital for a few days. We have to observe him, do a few tests, so we know what triggered it so that he doesn't have a relapse. Looking towards mom, "Mrs Sanghavi, has he had anything like this before?" Mom shook her head in response, "It is the first time doctor." "Well, don't worry, Sanjay is a strong kid. And you guys did the right thing by bringing him here. You are good parents!"

Mom and dad finally heaved a sigh of relief. Mom looked at Rajiv who was fast asleep on the couch in the waiting area. "I'll take him home; I'll call the school tomorrow and let them know that Sanjay will need some time off. I'll be back in the morning; you want me to get you anything, Arjun?" Dad kissed mom, "Good night! You get some rest. I'll see you in the morning."

I was hospitalised for exactly 12 days. I was injected with glucose since I couldn't bear to have the food at the hospital. But there was an upside of being in the hospital, I just loved the attention. Family friends, classmates, teachers, the principal, friends, everybody came to visit me. I felt special. I felt wanted. It was ironical how I felt sad when I was being discharged.

Dr Hwang walked dad and me to the elevator door, "Mr Sanghavi, as you are aware dust and pollen triggered the attack. This may occur again. Sanjay is now an asthmatic child, you will need to be careful of the surroundings he is in." Dr Hwang gave me a little pat on the head, "You were quite popular among the ladies here young man! You're going to grow up to be one helluva ladies man! Stay healthy son! We're going to miss you." I shook his hand and thanked him, just the way mom would expect me to.

As soon as I reached home, my brother Rajiv opened the door for us. Rajiv handed me a bunch of balloons and hugged me. "Welcome back home, bro!" I smiled. He then looked at me from head to toe and said "You've become really fat!" (I guess the glucose didn't do me any good. Why didn't I just stick to the hospital food?)

And my brother's statement was only the beginning of what I struggled with for many years to come. Obesity!

******

"We're going back home soon!" Rajiv and I interrupted our fight, looked towards mom and asked in unison "What?" "We're leaving for India soon!" mom responded. We thought mom was bluffing and this was just another innovative way she was adopting to break up our fight. Rajiv and I fought a lot and mom's statements of "Boogeyman is coming and getting you tonight if you don't stop fighting this instant!" or "I'm going to send you kids to boarding school!" didn't work anymore. Rajiv spoke first, "Didn't we just come back from India? We were there a few months ago!"

"We're going there for good now. We won't be coming back," mom responded in a serious tone. Brief silence followed. "I'm not leaving this place and you can't make me!" Rajiv stormed out of the room. I had recently begun to look up to my older brother and mirror him whenever I had the opportunity.

"Neither am I leaving!" said I and followed my brother out of the room. "Rajiv! Sanjay! Will you guys listen to me?" What followed this conversation was an eerie calm in the household. The house hadn't been that quiet in a long time.

Later that evening, mom walked into our bedroom while I was fast asleep. "Rajiv, can I come in?"

"I'm not going back to India! I like it here!"

"I know baby! Can I sit?"

Rajiv nodded.

"Rajiv, you know dad and I thought a lot before making this decision. In fact we wanted to leave for India last year. We delayed it because we knew how keen you were to attend secondary school here. So we decided we'd wait for you to complete fifth grade. Now since this academic year is coming to an end, we need to leave."

"But why? Why do we need to go?"

"Dad's company isn't doing too well. He says it may shut down in a couple of years. Plus things are getting too expensive. We can't afford it anymore. You understand, right?"

Rajiv nodded with a tear in his eye

"You're a big boy Rajiv and you've got to make your brother understand too. You'll help me convince him right?"

Rajiv nodded yet again and hugged mom "The school there will be as good as this one, won't it?"

"Of course baby, without doubt!" mom kissed Rajiv on the forehead, "Go to sleep now! You've got to wake up early for school!"

******

Convincing me wasn't too tough. "If you're going and Rajiv is going, what will I do here alone?" Those were my exact words.

The next thing I knew we were at the airport saying good bye to dad. "Why isn't dad coming along?" Rajiv asked mom. "He needs to wrap things up before he comes home. He can't just leave, can he now?" Rajiv ignored mom's response and ran to the book store in the airport lounge.

I followed my brother into the book store. Mom and dad looked at us and smiled at each other. "Take good care of yourself!" Mom told dad "Mona is going to be cooking for you the next few days till you find a maid." Rarely did dad get emotional but he actually choked up, "I'm going to miss you Geeta!" Mom got all teary-eyed and hugged dad, "We're doing this for the kids remember!" Dad nodded and said, "We'll survive this!"

From the book store I noticed the Mehta family approaching mom and dad. "Aunty Mona! Uncle Harish!" I ran towards them and jumped into Uncle Harish's arms. "Hey champ! All ready to fly, huh?" he asked. I nodded with glee. He placed me on the seat next to Sakhi.

Sakhi and I were quiet for a while. I kept staring at my shoes and finally murmured, "Are you going to miss me Sakhi?" She nodded shyly. I finally mustered the courage to have eye contact with her "I hope I get another best friend like you there! I'll tell her all about you! But how do I tell you about her?" That's the time it finally dawned on us. At a time when the Internet had not yet come into being, it was definitely going to be a task for us to keep in touch. Sakhi and I instantaneously hugged each other. We didn't have to say anything; it was like the end of an era for us.

******

Admission to a school in Bombay wasn't as tough as admission into Beverly American High. "Your nephew has scored an 'F' in physical education. That's definitely a concern area for me." Aunty Shaku - my dad's older sister and one of the city's most renowned lawyers looked the principal in the eye and said, "Father D'souza, you do know how many cases I've won for you and your school. If it weren't for me you would have been behind bars, for feeding *neem* leaves to your students!" Father D'souza a little flustered by the comment, quickly regained his composure "But, Mrs Shroff, he is your nephew after all, there is no concern at all." "Great! So, Father D'souza, when does Sanjay start?" "Well the academic year has already started a week ago, Monday sounds fine!" "Well Monday it is, then! Thank you Father!" Aunty Shaku walked out of the principal's office like she owned the room and hugged us as soon as she stepped out. She looked at mom, "Geeta! Sanjay can start school on Monday!" Mom began rambling "*Bhabhi* that was so quick! You're fantastic! How did you manage that?" While Mom continued to be in awe of aunty Shaku, I smiled and said, "Thanks *Bua*!"

******

"What's a uniform, mom?" I asked while I was getting ready for my first day at school. Mom responded while she helped me put my shorts on "It's the same dress code that all students in the school need to follow." "So, I'll have to wear this every day?" I asked sounding upset. "Yes. Now it's getting late. You don't want to be late on your first day at school right?"

Holding mom's hand I entered the big blue gate at St Vincent's High School. I distinctly remember there were at least a hundred boys wearing the same clothes as I was running around the school courtyard. I was so intimidated by the large crowd that from holding mom's hand, I slowly shifted to clinging on to her for dear life. "Don't be afraid!" she said while we climbed the stairs to get to my classroom on the second floor, "You'll do just fine!" I loved my mom, she could make any ugly situation sound comforting.

"Well, here we are!" When mom announced the arrival of our destination, I looked up at the board hung on the top of the door. It read, "Standard Third. Division B." As soon as I entered the classroom, there were exactly sixty one faces staring back at me not including the teachers. I was still holding on to mom's hand. From a centrally air conditioned classroom, with student-friendly chairs and desks which were the latest designs, colourful interiors, a white teacher and exactly 15 other students as classmates at Beverly American High, this was a rude culture shock for me. There were 61 students sitting in a space as large as my bedroom, the walls were coloured a bland white, the benches looked like they had been wrecked in a cyclone and the teacher had a wooden ruler in her hand. I looked towards mom. Mom signalled me to walk into the classroom. Couldn't she see the state of this classroom, how could she signal me to walk into this black hole? This wasn't a classroom; it was the devil's dungeon. I began wailing not wanting to leave mom's hand. I didn't want to step into that classroom. Somehow the teacher got me to let go of mom's hand and pulled me in. While I sobbed, the teacher looked towards the class, "Everybody this is Sanjay! It's his first day at school here today!" She shifted her gaze towards me, "Sanjay, go sit next to Hitesh for today!" She pointed towards a bench that already had three students sitting on it. And one of the students on that bench had a booger in his nose so large, that I almost puked at the sight of it. 'Boy! Oh Boy!' I thought to myself, was this going to be a long year ahead.

Today I am 13 years old.

It had been three months since my first day at school in the new academic year. I couldn't believe that I had not only completed but also survived four whole years at St Vincent's. It seemed like it was only yesterday that I was entering the big blue gate of the school holding mom's hand. I was now in the seventh standard.

Usually boys at the age of 13 are in the process of attaining puberty and look their ugliest best. And the unattractiveness quotient was quite prevalent among the boys in my class barring Siddharth Shukla. Siddharth, the only 14 year old in the class, was not successful in being promoted to the eighth standard the previous year and so was repeating the academic year. Siddharth looked like he was ready for the movies at 14. He was 5 feet 10 inches tall, fit, broad shouldered. With not a single zit or speck of unwanted hair on his face, he had sparkling white teeth and nice wavy hair. And boy! Did he smell good!

I, on the other hand, like all my other 13 year old classmates looked like a wreck. I weighed 75 kilograms (I was overweight by at least 15 kilograms), my chest was like a 15 year old girl's breasts; with zits all over my face I wore grandma spectacles and had a hair cut similar to that of the Bollywood heroes in the 1960's. Oh and how could I forget to mention my mannerisms! I was so effeminate at the time; my sway would have put Sridevi or Salma Hayek to shame.

Since all the taller boys had to occupy benches at the

back of the class, I fortunately or unfortunately had to sit right in front of Siddharth Shukla. Siddharth and I hardly spoke for the first three months since the academic year had begun. On the first day of the fourth month I heard an unfamiliar voice, "Sanjay, Could I borrow your eraser?" I turned around and saw Siddharth. Handing over my eraser I said "Of course! Here you go!" I continued "It's from Singapore!" He then gave me one of his million dollar smiles and thanked me. I then deliberately dropped my pencil on the ground. I bent to pick it up hoping Siddharth noticed my curves.

Suddenly, what I was doing dawned upon me; I came to my senses and sat up straight on the bench. Numerous questions were running in my head, "Why are you trying to impress him? Why do you keep smiling while talking to him? Why can't you stop thinking about him? Are you attracted to him?" Well in the coming couple of weeks I definitely did get an answer to my last question.

The 'eraser' incident helped break the ice and the two of us began talking. Siddharth and I progressed from being mere classmates to becoming friends.

Mrs Sethi, our mathematics teacher was teaching us the concept of simple interest and compound interest. While I tried hard to understand the concept, I suddenly felt an object slid down my spine. I turned around and saw Siddharth playing with a pencil in his hand. He winked at me, I smiled and mouthed the words "Stop it!" with a naughty grin on my face which really meant 'Continue doing it!' After a few minutes, I felt his hands on my back; he slowly brought it down to my ribs and finally was caressing my lower back. I was thoroughly enjoying the activity, I didn't object to it and he continued. I suddenly felt an erection. And it was definitely not the response I was hoping to get. Scared out of my wits, I pushed Siddharth's hands away and leaned in front out of his reach.

Even though I should have ideally been embarrassed by that incident, I surprisingly began looking forward to school every day. Not to learn new concepts or catch up with my friends but to be felt up by Siddharth. Being felt up by Siddharth was part of my daily routine now. However, the classes I would be felt up in varied. If Siddharth was bored he would fondle me in lenient Mrs Sethi's class and if he was in an adventurous mood he would feel me up in strict Mrs Mathur's class.

This continued for a few weeks till our Christmas break. Once our Christmas break was over, I returned to school only to find Siddharth missing for a couple of days. On enquiring, Mrs Sethi mentioned, "Siddharth has moved to the UK. He isn't going to be studying here anymore." After school that day, I stared for a good 15 minutes at the empty bench that once was occupied by Siddharth before I left for home.

It was strange after going through so much with Siddharth, as soon as he disappeared from my life; I continued to remain in denial of my sexuality and strongly believed that this was just a phase in my life that would eventually go away. Only I knew how wrong I was.

******

"As homework, could you all read chapter 17? I would want your thoughts on the two central characters mentioned in the text." Mrs Dickens rambled on and on about the usage of radiant words in certain passages and how we would be left flabbergasted at the end of the narrative. She continued "When it comes to English literature, expect the unexpected!" All I could focus on was the clock. It was Friday and there were exactly five minutes for school to end. Dad had promised to take me comic book shopping that weekend. "Happy reading!" is what I heard Mrs Dickens say last before the school bell rang. I began packing my bag and waved goodbye to my current best friend Saumil.

I was walking down the stairs at my slow pace when a group of boys from another section of the seventh standard ran past me. One of them briefly looked at me and suddenly announced to one of his pals, "*Oye Shohaib! Goodhve ke bable dekho!*" (Hey Shohaib! Look at the faggot's boobs!) At that time, I had felt a bag of mixed feelings. I was stunned, anxious, shocked, petrified all at the same time. In unison all of them circled around me and yelled, "*Bade Bade! Bade Bade!*" (Big ones! Big ones!) I thought the best thing to do at that moment was ignore them and walk away. And that is exactly what I did. Thankfully they did not follow me or stop me. On my way home, I began thinking about the chances of me bumping into them in a school with over 1000 students. I consoled myself by saying "never!" again and again to myself.

My optimism was killed the following Monday.

As soon as school ended that Monday, I began walking down the usual flight of stairs. And what did I see? The group of bullies standing against the wall waiting for me. I believe every group of bullies follows the same hierarchy - There is one leader, one right hand man (always the best friend of the leader) and the rest - flunkies. This group of bullies that I encountered had a similar hierarchy. The group was led by Jigar; his right hand man was Shohaib and there were two other sidekicks whose names I do not remember. One look at Jigar and you knew that this was the kind of guy your mother would not want you to be friends with. He had a stubble, always had the first two buttons of his shirt open and his breath smelled of eggs. Jigar greeted me, "*Kyun goodhve? Kaisa hain?*" (So faggot, how are you?) I knew this was not going to be my day. Ignoring the group, I looked the other way and began walking. "Fuck'n Faggot! We're talking to you!" said Shohaib. "Me?" I asked innocently. "Yeah you! Fatso!" said the sidekicks in unison.

"You think one of us looks like a fat faggot?" asked Jigar.

I nodded my head and said "No!"

"So, what bra size do you wear?"

"I don't wear a bra. I wear a vest."

"A vest for the breast I see!"

The statement was followed by unanimous laughter. I looked down and asked submissively, "Can I go?"

"Sure!" Jigar responded.

As soon as I was beginning to leave, Jigar fondled my chest. As an immediate reflex, I pushed his hand away.

His group of friends pinned me down to the ground, "Big mistake! Fatso!" I heard Shohaib say. I began crying and yelled, "Let me go! Let me go!" I was fondled for a good 15 minutes by the gang of boys. While one fondled the others chanted, "*Bade Bade! Bade Bade!*" (Big ones! Big ones!) Every gang member took a turn to fondle my chest. "*Goodh ke kapde utarva dete hain aur phir uske bable dabate hain!*" (Let's get the Faggot's clothes off and then press his boobs) I heard one of them say. All that time, I struggled to let go. I screamed for help. I prayed. None of it was helping. I just laid there helplessly being molested by a group of boys. Suddenly, "*Kya kar rahe ho tum log*?" (What are you doing?) It was the school peon. The boys left me where I was and ran all the way towards the exit without looking back. The peon just looked at my tear-streaked face and with no sympathy at all said, "*Ghar Jao!*" (Go Home!)

As soon as I reached home, mom looked at my crumpled muddy shirt and enquired, "What happened?" "Nothing!" I responded. "Then how did your shirt get so dirty?" "Oh that! We were playing football today." Immediately after my response, I thought to myself, "Sports and I? What kind of a silly excuse was that! Mom is definitely going to rubbish my alibi." And subconsciously, I was hoping mom would call my bluff and probe. I wanted to let my heart out. I wanted to tell her how a bunch of nasty boys stayed after school to rag me and pick on me, how they hurt me, how I struggled, how I screamed, all of it. But all mom said in response to my excuse was, "Hmmm! Go and get out of those dirty clothes quickly! Make sure you take a bath! I've made some *Samosas*. I'll serve them when you're ready." I nodded, went to my bedroom and shut the door behind me.

I removed my clothes and stood naked in front of the mirror. I saw a few bruises on my chest and shoulder. When I touched the bruises it pained. I began staring at my reflection in the mirror. For the first time in my life, I hated what I saw. I began to see what everybody else saw - 'A Fat Faggot!' Suddenly, the incident with the gang of boys flashed before my eyes. I began to cry. I fell down on my knees and broke down. I wanted to howl so bad but I didn't. I just couldn't let mom know, she would be devastated.

I took a shower and stepped out of the bathroom. Before I could put my clothes on, I prayed. I prayed never to be ragged again, I prayed never to bump into those boys again, I prayed to be more masculine, I prayed not to be gay, I prayed to be a healthy fit boy who didn't suffer from obesity or asthma. Surprisingly I prayed for everything except the strength to face my tormentors. I feel God was listening to rock music when I said this prayer. It went unheard.

The ragging just didn't stop. I was ragged not just for the days to come but in fact for the next few years till I completed secondary school. Well at least there were different groups that ragged me (as the saying goes 'variety is the spice of life'), I was also privileged to experience different forms of ragging.

I cringed to go to school every single day.

******

"Sanjaaaay!" I looked in the direction my name was hollered from. I saw nothing. "Oh! Sanjaaaay!" I heard my name being called out again. The room was empty. The door was locked. 'Who is calling for me?' I wondered. Bizarrely, I felt like the voice came from the mirror placed on the left wall of my bedroom. I walked towards the mirror cautiously and slowly peered into it. I squealed in my head at the reflection I saw.

I saw an image of a donkey's head placed on an obese teenage boy's body. The boy wore a court jester's suit and held up a placard that read, "FAGGOT!" I instantly ran to the corner of my room and crouched up against the wall.

"Sanjaaaay! You ugly piece of blubber!" I heard voices again. I dropped my head between my knees, closed my ears and screamed, "Go away! Let me be!" The voices got louder, "Sanjay! You fat fuck'n faggot!" I screamed louder, "Aaaaarrrggghhhhh!" I continued screaming till I was sure that my cry had overpowered the voices in the room. Finally, they stopped. I gradually opened my eyes, moved my hands away from my ears, wiped my tears and vowed never to look into the mirror again. I began living in the constant fear of being me.

I started looking to food for comfort. Cheese sandwiches, chicken burgers, french-fries, ice-cream, chocolates rapidly became my best friends. They were my inner circle now. When I was sad I looked at the bar of snickers in my hand, "Today Mrs Mathur has given us an awful lot of homework to do." When I was angry I looked to the plate of french-fries, "Today Jigar pinned me down on the school's toilet floor." And surprisingly, I looked at Dollops ice-cream even when I felt the rare sentiment of happiness and felt happy

I began putting on more weight. I started doing badly at school.

"What's wrong Sanjay? Your grades are falling! Look at Rajiv, he is doing so well. Why can't you be like him?" mom said. I was tired of the constant comparison with my oh-so-brilliant brother. "Because I am not him! I'm a different person!" I responded evidently pissed off. "Sanjay! Stop being a smart alec!" I stormed out of the hall and moved to the room where my brother, Rajiv was sitting.

"What's wrong Fatso?" My brother asked. "It's none of your business and stop calling me that! I have a name." I snapped back.

"You want to play cricket?" My brother enquired trying to change the topic.

"No!"

"How about table tennis?"

"No!"

"What do you want to do then?"

"Nothing! The Miss India Contest is going to be shown on TV, I want to watch that!"

"You're such a faggot! You never want to play any sports. How I wish I had a real boy as a brother!"

"What? What did you just say?"

Rajiv paid no heed and walked out of the room. And he didn't have to repeat what he just said. The message was loud and clear.

******

Home is the place a kid my age should feel secure. It should be the place he wants to come back to every single day. In my case, it was a little different, coming home was beginning to seem like a continuation of the ragging I was facing at school. I began to feel claustrophobic.

Be it at school or at home, life was becoming a struggle for me and I didn't want to live anymore. I would look at the view from my balcony window and imagine myself falling to the ground; I would look at the knife placed on the kitchen sink and picture the blood of my veins on it; I would look at the ceiling fan and visualize my body hanging from the core with a rope tied around my neck.

I came back home from school to find Aunty Shaku seated on the couch. "Hello *Bua*!" I greeted her touching her feet. "Hi Sanjay! We were just talking about you!"

"You were?" I curiously asked

Aunty Shaku shifted her gaze to my mother, "So you were saying….."

"What do I do *Bhabhi*? His chest doesn't seem like it's going to stop growing. I'm worried!"

"Is it a chest or a breast?" Rajiv who was also seated there and very much part of the conversation snickered.

I gave Rajiv a snarling look when he said that. I was appalled that my chest was a topic of discussion and that too with Aunty Shaku present. I was even more appalled by *Bua's* response to my mother's concern.

"Start making him wear a bra!" Aunty Shaku said.

"Come on *Bhabhi*!" mom smiled.

Why is mom smiling?. I'm supposed to find solace at home and not frivolous discussion around my chest. I couldn't bear to hear anymore of the conversation so I stormed into my bedroom shutting the door behind me.

Looking up in the direction of the sky, I yelled,

"Happy?" and began to cry. I found it easy to blame my current misery on God.

The very next day, I was on my way to Dr Agarwal's clinic with mom in tow. Aunty Shaku advised Mom yesterday saying I should be checked for female hormones in my body and hence referred us to Dr Agarwal.

At the clinic, I was staring at the Body Mass Index chart on the wall. It was pretty evident from the poster that I was currently overweight by exactly 25 kilograms. "Sanjay! Come sit down here!" Mom called out to me. I went and sat next to her. Just then, "Mrs Sanghavi" the nurse called out, "Doctor will see you now!"

I walked into the doctor's cabin following mom. "Hello doctor!" mom greeted him. "Hello Mrs Sanghavi, Mrs Shroff mentioned that you would be coming." Placing her hand on my back, mom said "This is my son Sanjay! We needed to check...." mom began hesitating. The doctor interrupted seeing mom hesitate, "Yes! Yes! Mrs Shroff told me about the problem" then looking at me he said "Sanjay, son, come sit on the bed!" I did as I was told without saying a word. "Will you remove your shirt?" As soon as I removed my shirt, Dr Agarwal started pressing his finger into my chest at different spots. "Hmmmm" he said. "What is it doctor?" mom enquired. Sanjay will need to do a few tests and then I will tell you what the problem is. It definitely could be female hormones though." As soon as he said that, I visualised myself as a clown in the middle of the circus being mocked at. I snapped out of my thought rather quickly when I heard mom say "We'll get these tests done and bring the results back to you." "Definitely" the doctor responded.

On our way back home from Dr Agarwal's clinic, I finally had the courage to tell mom what I had been meaning to tell her for a long time now. The depression I was going through was beginning to take a toll on me and so I instantaneously asked mom, "Could I see a psychologist?" "What?" mom was definitely taken aback. "I just think I need to see a psychologist." I continued. Well it was finally proven that mom came from an old school of thought which said that going to a psychologist is a waste of money and time since they don't diagnose or cure any problems; only crazy people went to psychologists. Mom's response to my request was, "What rubbish! There is no need! There is nothing wrong with you!" That was the first and the last time I ever brought such a request to mom again.

My test results came through and just as I assumed there were no female hormones. I was like I expected to be: 'All Man' and a fighter at that! I just hoped my family would begin to see it too.

Today I am 16 years old.

I was ecstatic today. I had just appeared for the last paper of my secondary school examinations. I was going to apply for junior college that year. This meant I wasn't going to ever encounter Jigar or Shohaib or any of those nincompoops that ragged me again. As soon as I reached home, I hugged mom and did a little dance for her, jiggling my belly. "How was your exam?" she enquired. "Who cares?" I screamed happily "No more school! Woo-hoo!" "But junior college admissions are not so easy. You remember how Rajiv struggled with admission in spite of scoring so high." I just nodded pretending to listen to every word mom was saying. I quickly turned around to tiptoe into my bedroom when mom wasn't looking and murmured 'Killjoy!'

Dad came back home with a bunch of pamphlets that evening. A closer look at the pamphlets and it was obvious we were planning a family holiday. Correction! We weren't planning the holiday, the holiday was already planned. Dad asked all of us to gather around the center table. "We leave next Friday and we'll be back the following Thursday!" Handing over one of the pamphlets to mom, dad said, "Look at the hotel we're staying at! Isn't it beautiful?"

I knew how much mom hated to travel and it was obvious when she tried to please dad in such situations. Without any eye contact with dad, mom exclaimed, "It's lovely!" I wondered how dad could not see through the bad acting. Mom would definitely have won a *razzie* for that performance.

"But where are we going?" I asked

Rajiv butted in, "Thailand! Dumb-ass! Didn't you know that?"

And this was just one of the many important family activities that I was never involved in while the decisions were being made. In conversation with my parents that night I also got to know that this wasn't just going to be a family trip for us but for eight other families we had never seen in our life. This was going to be a group tour.

The next day while dad was away at work, Rajiv complained to mom, "Group tour! How could dad get us registered on a group tour? Come on mom! We'll have to follow stupid timings, wake up early, go for boring bus rides and speak to a bunch of losers!" "Now, now, Rajiv you don't even know these people, how can you call them a bunch of losers already. I've taught you better than being judgmental" Mom responded calmly. I would have chosen to be a silent spectator but the last thing I wanted was to give another group of strangers an opportunity to mock me. I was now intimidated by large groups since the ragging incidents. "I agree with Rajiv, mom! It's a stupid idea. I think we should talk to dad and cancel the holiday."

Well without doubt, our suggestions were paid no heed to and the following Friday we were in the plane on our way to Bangkok with a tour leader and eight other families.

******

Seven days went by and we were at the Mumbai airport bidding good bye to all our new found friends. It was strange how all of us in the family had different takeaways from the trip. Dad came back with the thought that he had provided his family the best vacation of their life; mom came back with the worry of how much money was spent on this holiday; I was back with an addiction to the inhaler on having an asthma attack in Bangkok and Rajiv was back with new found love.

Mahi Chopra, a pretty 18-year-old medical student accompanied by her mom and nephew were one of the families on the group tour. She was petite with nice long hair and a wide smile. Your first impression of Mahi would be that of a warm, friendly person with a down to earth attitude.

Mahi and I got along like a house on fire. We had the same taste in movies, music, books and food. All through the trip I wished I had a sister like her rather than a brother like Rajiv. Mahi and Rajiv hardly spoke on the trip. The only time they did speak resulted in a heated argument by the end of it.

"I think doctors are given more credit than they deserve." Rajiv had initiated a conversation while Mahi and I were discussing the latest Alanis Morisette, 'single in the hotel lawn'.

"Excuse me?" Mahi responded

"I said I think doctors are...."

"I heard what you said. What did you mean by that?"

"I mean, doctors get paid for what they do and they better save a life, why give them God like status for saving lives?"

"Do you know how much research and days of reading are involved for each patient? Do you know what the average number of patients treated by a doctor on a daily basis is? Do you know what kind of detailed skill is required by a surgeon in an emergency room?"

"I agree that doctors invest a lot of time and effort in the kind of work they do, but so does Mukesh Ambani as an entrepreneur or Shahrukh Khan as an actor. So again, I repeat, why give doctors god-like status for just doing their job?"

"You're comparing Shahrukh Khan to a doctor? You think Shahrukh Khan should be given god-like status over doctors who spend all their lives finding a cure to cancer or AIDS?"

"Hey! I never said Shahrukh Khan should be given god-like status but he is quite the entertainer. I got rid of a splitting headache just by watching one of his movies."

"You think that's funny? Not to me... Just goes to show how oblivious and ignorant you are as a person...."

"Me? Oblivious? Ignorant? At least I'm not one-dimensional, try being open to another person's point of view sometimes...."

And that one random statement from Rajiv triggered the most boring debate on the trip. I remember only the two of them being left after fifteen minutes of that conversation. Everyone around them had moved away from their vicinity including me. The discussion then went on for many hours after that. It ended only with disgust and more disgust on their faces.

"This isn't going anywhere! You're a waste of my time. Continue being your unaware self!" Mahi snapped at Rajiv.

"Yeah! And you can carry on being your closed minded self!" Rajiv retaliated.

They never spoke on the trip after that.

"Are you awake?" Rajiv asked me. I was pooped after the long flight and horrendous cab ride back home and only wanted to sleep. The last thing I wanted was to have a conversation with my brother. I chose to ignore my brother's question so that he thought I was asleep. But he continued, "You liked Mahi?" I was so fond of Mahi and did not mind conversing if it was about her with my brother. With my eyes now wide awake I responded "Yeah! She would have been a fun sister! Why do you ask?"

"I think she is really cute" said Rajiv.

"But..." I was interrupted.

"Yeah! We had that stupid argument. But the passion in her eyes during that argument was killer, man!"

"So? What is the point you're trying to make?"

"Don't you get it dumbass?"

"If you want to call me a dumbass, then I do not want to have this conversation."

"I'm sorry. Please listen to me."

That was the first time my brother was trying to have a conversation with me. I felt superior, suddenly it seemed like I had the upper hand I had the control.

"OK! go on...." I said commandingly.

"I saw Mahi and you were having so much fun on the trip, it left me envious."

"Why?"

"I think I really like her."

"So? What's the big deal?"

"I think I really, really like her!"

"Ohhhh!" I reacted, I finally got it. My brother was in love with Mahi. I liked Mahi so much that the thought of her being around more because of my brother left me unintentionally happy. At the same time, I was surprised my brother trusted me with that kind of information. It felt kind of weird and special at the same time. My brother never thought of me as a confidant before. This meant my brother was beginning to trust me and that made me not only trust him back but even respect him.

Ironically, the very next day Mahi called telling me that she thought Rajiv was cute and liked him. I thought this was meant to be and did what every faithful brother would do in a situation like this. I passed on Mahi's message to Rajiv. Rajiv asked Mahi out that weekend and they met at an *Udupi* (type of Indian restaurant) for a *dosa* (delicacy from the southern part of India). And this was the beginning of their beautiful relationship.

******

Yesterday.... All my troubles seemed so far away.... Now it looks as though they're here to stay........

I was listening to Beatles. "Hey Sanjay!" a familiar voice interrupted. I turned around to find Rajiv leaning against the door. Unplugging my walkman, I greeted him back. "Hey! What's up? Weren't you meeting Mahi today?"

"Na. She's got a few extra classes. So we're not catching up today...."

"Oh... Ok"

"Listen, I was wondering, there is this Indian adaptation of CATS playing tonight at Agni. Wanna go?"

Rajiv is asking me to go watch a musical with him. If anybody hated musicals, it had to be Rajiv. I remember when dad mistakenly took the two of us to watch Hema Malini perform the story of *Ramayana;* Rajiv received a lot of unwanted attention for his loud yawning. And to top it all, when the lady on Rajiv's right requested him to stop yawning, he retaliated, "Basanti was an item in *Sholay*!" And with that comment piercing the entire auditorium (Yes! My brother was loud), Hema Malini walked off the stage in the middle of her performance. We, on the other hand were asked to leave the auditorium immediately and had to brave the angry glare of 497 pairs of eyes on us. I wish I had a camera at the time; my dad's red face was definitely worthy of the front page in the newspaper.

"You! A musical! With me! Are you sure Rajiv? You do remember what happened at the musical a couple of years ago right?" I responded to my brother's surprising request. "And I am in no mood to embarrass myself," I continued.

"Come on Sanjay! I was 12 then...." Rajiv smiled clearly remembering the incident from the recent past.

"Correction! 15!" I laughed.

"Yeah! Yeah! I know! That was hilarious! But, I swear I'll behave this time. I know how much you love musicals. Plus I get to spend some quality time with you. For a change, let's do something you want. Also, there is this awesome *vada-pav* (Indian snack) joint I've discovered outside Agni. I'll treat you to that after the show."

I smiled. And of course, I readily agreed to the plan. I felt like I was going to cry happy tears. I always thought my brother was embarrassed to be seen in public with me. How wrong was I? Here Rajiv was initiating something that was of interest to me and wanted to be a part of it himself.

Evidently, the relationship between Mahi and Rajiv was also the start for another beautiful relationship - The one between Rajiv and me.

******

Saumil and I looked at the list put up on the notice board. After browsing through approximately 100 names

I finally read 'Sanjay Sanghavi' and heaved a sigh of relief. I left Saumil in the crowd around the display board and stood in a place where I could breathe again. After a few minutes, Saumil rushed towards me giving me a high five. "We made it bro!" Saumil my best friend of many years and I finally made it to Junior College. We were going to be first year junior college students at MD College of Arts and Commerce.

As usual, I was a wreck before the first day of college. I was so nervous that I had to relieve myself at least five times every half hour. Senior students ragging junior students in the first week of college is common and I was sure I would be picked on. I wasn't as effeminate as I was in school but the weight gain just didn't stop. I weighed 105 kilos at the time making me overweight by a good 30 to 35 kilograms.

To my surprise I didn't get ragged; I felt a lot of respite when I was seated in the lecture room without being picked on by a single senior student on my way to college. It was only later during the course of the academic year that I got to know from a few senior students that I didn't get picked on because they thought I was a parent of one of the students in the college.

Two weeks had passed since college started and I was just about finding my feet. College was a completely different experience from school. Nobody cared whether I was fat or thin, effeminate or non effeminate, rich or poor. I liked going to college, I knew this was the place I would be able to regain my lost confidence.

Saumil and I always occupied the third last bench in the class and we were more or less surrounded by the same people every day. All of us began talking and it was only a matter of time that we became a group of friends that always hung out together. We liked calling ourselves the gang and were definitely a diverse group of people. The group had: Saumil, my old-time schoolmate who was suddenly obsessed with physical fitness; Javed, a conservative religious Muslim; Saif, non-conservative non-religious Muslim; Joanna, daddy's little girl still in the process of finding herself, Rakhi, a walking-talking fashion fiesta and shopaholic; and of course me. Oh! And how could I forget Rukhsat Abir.

Rukhsat was one of the most stunning women I have ever met. She really seemed like one of god's chosen apples dropped from heaven. When she walked her pear shaped butt swayed, her hair blew in the wind and her eyes twinkled. All the guys in the group were awestruck by her presence. But not me, Rukhsat and I became very close friends over a period of time. We sat next to each other in class, we studied together, we laughed together, we ate together, we spoke for hours on the phone every single day. With the pressure of social norms in my head, I thought this was love.

"I think I'm in love!" I proclaimed while Saumil, Javed and Saif looked at me in astonishment. We were all at Saumil's house doing what boys do - discussing women and talking sex.

"What?" Saumil asked "With whom?"

"You like Joanna, don't you?" Javed asked with optimism. Javed had a crush on Rukhsat himself and was hoping deep down in his heart I wouldn't say Rukhsat.

Saif highly impatient questioned, "So who the fuck is it?"

"Rukhsat!" I sighed

Saumil exclaimed "Rukhsat! You mean our Rukhsat! Are you blind? You can do better than Rukhsat for sure!" Astonished by Saumil's exclamation I only got to know a few months later that he, like Javed, had a crush on Rukhsat and so was trying to dissuade me.

Javed on the other hand continued to remain quiet.

Saif, the only one among the four of us who didn't have anything at stake because he, luckily, did not have a crush on Rukhsat responded like I was expecting any friend to react. "Dude! Go for it!" he said.

I chose not to say anything to Rukhsat till a week before her birthday. Rukhsat hadn't come to college that day and I was sharing the bench with Joanna and Rakhi for a change during the French lecture. Everybody attended a coaching class for the subject so no one ever bothered to listen to the lecturer in class. The lecturer knew that and so didn't care whether any of the students actually listened to her or not. Joanna and Rakhi giggled away while the lecture was on and I could not help but intrude into their conversation. "What are you girls giggling about?" I asked. "We were talking about Rukhsat's crush" answered Rakhi. On hearing Rukhsat's name and the word 'crush' my eyes widened and I curiously asked the girls, "What about her crush?" "Rukhsat has had a huge crush on Saumil right from day one since college started" Joanna replied. "Really?" I was devastated; I felt like the devil had ripped my heart, picked up my blood-spattered soul and was laughing at me while I fell to my knees.

I knew I had to speak to Rukhsat. I called her that evening and told her we had to speak urgently and that I would tell her about it after college the next day.

Rukhsat and I were in the college library. Seeing the anxiety on my face she held my hand and asked, "What is wrong Sanjay? What is so urgent?" I looked at her big brown eyes and strongly believed that I was in love with this woman. It was strange how I never felt the physical attraction towards Rukhsat, how I never had the urge to hold her tight and caress her, how I never wanted to kiss her. All I had with Rukhsat was an unexplainable emotional connection and that for me was love. "Tell me Sanjay, you're spooking me out by being so quiet" Rukhsat probed. "You and I have known each other for a few months now" I began "How come you never told me you had a crush on Saumil?" Rukhsat laughed and said "That was the urgency? Come on Sanjay, we girls were just having a little bit of fun. It isn't that I'm in love with Saumil." I was relieved and I thought that this was the best opportunity to declare my unsure love for Rukhsat. "I really love you Rukhsat!" Rukhsat was definitely shocked by the statement. "Huh?" she responded. And then I asked her something that I should never have asked: "Do you love me?" Rukhsat in the curtest tone replied, "NO!" Spontaneously my next question was, "Is it because I'm fat!" She collected her books and began to walk away. "Rukhsat! Wait!" I called out to her. It was too late, she was already gone.

Rukhsat and I never spoke after that. The following month Rukhsat left for the United States. In spite of my group of friends telling me that Rukhsat had always planned to go abroad for her further studies and it was only coincidental that she left at a time when I let out my feelings to her, I kept blaming myself for her leaving. As soon as she was gone I realised that I never did love her as my lover but only loved her as a friend, as a confidant, as an unconventional soul mate. The realisation, however, came a tad too late.

******

I hadn't seen Saumil for days. He wasn't responding to my calls either. I sat next to Joanna in class and asked her, "Where the fuck has Saumil been?" Joanna shook her head saying she didn't know. She continued paying attention to the lecturer in class. "Should we go to his place? I'm kind of worried." "Shhh!" placing her finger on her lips Joanna asked me to shut up. After class that day, all of us did decide to pay a visit to Saumil's place.

"Come in guys!" Saumil's mom opened the door to us "Saumil is in the bedroom." All of us went in and I yelled as soon as I entered, "What the fuck! Saumil where have you been? We've been worried sick!" Rakhi continued, "And you're wearing Nike tracks, a Benetton Shirt, so you're definitely not ill." Joanna rubbished Rakhi's statement "Because people who are ill wear Reebok tracks and an Adidas tee?" "Will you girls shut up and let Saumil speak." Saif redirected the conversation to where it was supposed to head.

"Nothing guys! My cousins were here and I was with them. So I took a few days off. No big deal!" Saumil responded as a matter of fact.

"Why the fuck weren't you taking calls then?" I quickly interrogated.

"I was just busy." Saumil responded coldly.

All of us spent about an hour at Saumil's place when Javed reminded all of us, "Guys it is getting late. I think it's time for us to leave."

Saumil and I had been friends for close to 6 years now. I knew him better than that. I knew there was something wrong. He seemed cold and distant. I decided to stay back after the rest of the gang left.

"So what is wrong?" I asked

"Nothing" he responded

"Come on Saumil! You can tell me the truth."

Saumil looked at me from head to toe, "You remember Prakriti."

"Your cousin right?" I responded vaguely remembering what she looked like "I met her briefly while she was here a couple of weeks ago. Sweet girl."

"Prakriti spoke to me after meeting you. And she told me that if I hung out with you too often I would never get a girlfriend."

"That is why you were avoiding me?" I concluded.

Saumil didn't say anything after that. He just waited for me to leave. And that is exactly what I did.

Walking home, I began introspecting. I thought college was going to be the place that I would build my lost confidence. I guess I was wrong. Hearing that statement from my best friend of many years did not only make me hate myself all over again, I was on the verge of losing faith in all relationships.

My confidence continued to drop, however my friends didn't let me lose trust in them. I narrated the incident to the rest of the gang. After that, Saumil didn't just lose me as a friend; he lost 4 other great friends. The loyalty of my friends pleasantly surprised me. I promised myself that day I would die for Joanna, Rakhi, Javed and Saif if I had to.

Today I am 18 years old.

While I was reading a comic book I was distracted by a voice that broke the silence in the room. "Geeta, don't you think it would be a good idea if Sanjay registered for some activity during the holidays rather than sitting like a log all day long?" dad asked mom while he sipped his morning cup of tea. "Look at him, he has only been sleeping or eating or watching television the entire day. This won't do him any good."

Dad chose not to acknowledge that I was actually sitting in the same room as them while he had this conversation with mom. And after that strong statement, mom had no choice but to agree. "I think it is a good idea. You have anything in mind?" Mom responded like a diligent wife to dad's concern. Dad handed the newspaper to mom pointing to an advertisement. Mom read it aloud "Public speaking classes at the Society of Learning and Development"

"Mom! Do I have to go for these stupid public speaking classes?" I whined to mom in the kitchen after dad left for work. "Sanjay, it is just a seven day course. The days will pass in a jiffy. You won't even realise how time flew. Do this for your dad, please." Mom responded trying to provide me some solace.

Well in my home, when dad made the decision there was little you could do to reverse it. Dad came home that evening and handed me a receipt from the Society of Leaning and Development. "Sanjay, take this along with you on your first day of class. You start on Monday." I didn't even have the time to react, dad walked away after handing the slip to me.

The following Monday, I kissed mom goodbye and headed to the Society of Learning and Development for my first day of class. Since it was my first time travelling alone to the other part of town, I left earlier than required. I was really bad with directions and was sure that I would lose my way. Surprisingly, I did not and was the first student to make it to class.

There was at least a half hour for the class to begin. Mr Vaidyanathan the course instructor - was already present in the classroom and was immersed in reading a book. Mr Vaidyanathan was a tall elderly man in his 60's. He seemed like an intimidating intellectual when you saw him from a distance but came across as affectionate as soon as he made eye contact. I went up to the third row to take a seat. Mr Vaidyanathan looked up from his book, smiled and greeted me, "Welcome son!" Just as I was about to take a seat, he asked me "What is your name, son?" "Sanjay. Sanjay Sanghavi." I replied. "Sanjay, could you do me a huge favour?" I nodded like an obedient student. "Could you stand at the entrance and greet everybody who comes in with a smile?" Surprised at his eccentric request, I stood by the door to greet every student that came in. "Weirdo!" I whispered to myself.

I was an 18-year-old college student but looked at least twice my age because of my weight. Every time I did greet a student entering, I would either receive a smile from the person I greeted or I would receive a "Hello sir!" in response. These students thought I was the course lecturer. "This isn't doing too much for my already low self esteem," I thought to myself. When there were exactly two minutes for the class to start, Mr Vaidyanathan signalled me to come in and take a seat.

Mr Vaidyanathan started speaking. For a man his age, he had a loud commanding powerful voice just like Amitabh Bachchan "Before I start with the course, I would like everybody to applaud Sanjay. Sanjay was such a good sport to greet each of you with a smile." I enjoyed the applause. I felt important. Like always, I loved being the centre of attention.

Mr. Vaidyanathan ensured that all of us were seated next to complete strangers, these were people we didn't know from Adam. I exchanged pleasantries with the people sitting next to me, immediately after which Mr. Vaidyanathan began, "One smile can make such a difference, and not only to your life but to the life of others and that is the very reason that Sanjay was asked to greet each of you with a smile this morning." While he spoke, I nodded vigorously agreeing with every word he said. Since I truly believed what was spoken, I made sure I listened attentively over the next 7 days.

After a series of 42 introductions and a few motivating words from Mr. Vaidyanathan on day-1 of the course, he ended the class with a statement that is etched in my mind till date, "Love yourself for who you are! Everybody comes with their own pros and cons; it's the way you look at yourself that eventually matters."

I repeated those words to myself in my head on the way home. While I was seated in the train, some of my co-passengers looking in my direction were staring and snickering. I was used to that kind of reaction from complete strangers because of my struggle with weight. But that day, instead of thinking these people were laughing at me, I strongly believed that they were laughing with me. I looked them in the eye and gave a broad smile. And guess what? They stopped snickering and smiled back.

I decided to convert my learning into action at home as well. Sitting on the couch, dad grouchily switched channels while watching television. I went up to him and spontaneously hugged him. Dad smiled.

"How was your day?" he asked me as he switched off the television.

"It was great! Thanks so much for forcing me to register for the course. I'm anticipating a lot of good learning."

"I'm glad you're enjoying it. I wish we had courses like these in our time. I would have been a better person."

"Dad, I think you turned out just fine."

That night, dad and I had the longest conversation we ever had had in the past.

I was thrilled. Three rarities happened for me that day. Firstly, dad smiled. Secondly, dad initiated conversation with me. Thirdly, I strongly felt a sense of accomplishment.

******

I was awakened by the loud ring of my phone. "Sanjay! It's me Joanna!" Joanna and I had become really good friends over the years and we were currently at that stage in our friendship where we could call each other at any time of the day without feeling apologetic about it. "Joanna, it's 7 am! What do you want?" I enquired sounding pissed. "I had this weird feeling today…. I think I dreamt it….. Something really good is going to happen to you so I had to call and let you know" Joanna said excitedly. "You woke me up for this?" I hung up on Joanna and went back to sleep.

I woke up after a few hours realising that it was only a couple of hours for the class to begin. Mr. Vaidyanathan was very particular about time and there was no way I would want to reach late for his lecture. I had begun enjoying his classes so much that I always made sure I made it to class way before time. I browsed through the clothes in my cupboard and picked up the only tee-shirt I had.

It had been exactly three years since I had worn a tee in public. I was so embarrassed by the way the shape of my body showed when I wore a T-shirt that I always stuck to wearing shirts. I didn't know what got into me that day to make the decision of actually wearing a tee. It was surprising to me at first, but a little bit of self-introspection made me realize that this could only mean a positive change for me.

I just about made it in time for class. Mr. Vaidyanathan had just asked one of my classmates to come to the front of the room and sing 'Hero' by Mariah Carey. I never listen to the lyrics of a song but that day I did.

And then a hero comes along
With the strength to carry on
You cast your fears aside
And you know you can survive
So when you feel like hope is gone
Look inside you and be strong
Coz you finally see the truth
That a hero lies in you...

I knew I was inspired.

During the tea break, like an excited 10- year- old child I walked up to Mr. Vaidyanathan and said, “Sir, look I'm wearing a T-shirt!" Mr. Vaidyanathan did not seem the least bit flustered or surprised by my random comment. He smiled at me and responded, “That's fantastic Sanjay! I'm so proud of you." With my head held up high, I went to get myself a well deserved cup of tea.

Post the break, Mr. Vaidyanathan made a strange request, “Now, I need each one of you to come up here and share your learning from the course so far." Everybody was taken aback by the request, including me. ‘What will I say up there? I've learnt so much but how do I put it together in a one minute extempore speech?' I thought to myself.

But when my turn did come to speak, I didn't know why I was worried. Whatever I had to say surprisingly came naturally to me. “My parents forced me to register for this class," I began. “I didn't think this course would do anything for me. I thought this would be nothing but a complete waste of my free time during the holidays. But just these three days of class have proved me wrong. Sir's words - 'Love yourself for who you are' keep drumming in my head all the time now. Every time I walked the street and people stared at me, I always concluded these strangers were trying to tell me something that translated as ‘Look at the fat Ox!' or ‘Look at the eighth wonder of the world!' But...." I could sense that I was tearing up, I began crying. I knew these were nothing but tears of triumph. This was a triumph over a fight that I was having with myself for all these years. It was at that very moment I realised that this course was not just a regular public speaking course but a life changing experience. In spite of choking up, I continued speaking "But today if anybody stares at me, I know they are only looking because they are envious of my good looks." There was a pleasant giggle among the audience. "This course is a new beginning for me" I concluded. And with that statement I walked off the podium to a thunderous applause smiling at Mr Vaidyanathan with a complete sense of gratitude.

On reaching home, I sat in my bedroom alone; I stared at the mirror from a distance not directly peering into it. I kept asking myself, 'Should I? Shouldn't I?' Gathering as much courage as I could, I walked towards the mirror. Standing in front of it with my eyes closed, I saw flashes of a donkey's head, a court jester's suit, a teenage boy's obese body, a placard reading "FAGGOT". My head began re-playing the voices I had heard exactly 5 years ago, "You ugly piece of blubber!" "You fat fuck'n faggot"! "You good for nothing moron!" I held back tears and slowly opened my eyes. For the first time in many years I saw me. No donkey's head, no court jester's suit, no placard and no voices. Just me. I slowly started running my fingers down my reflection on the mirror. I ran my fingers down the reflection of my eyes, my nose, my lips, my body. 'So that is what I look like?' I thought to myself. I felt a tear roll down my cheek. I was happy. I liked what I saw. It was evident that the many years of self hatred were changing to hope.

I immediately called Joanna, "Hey!" she said on answering the phone. "You were right! Something good did happen to me today" I told her. "What? What happened?" she asked with utmost curiosity. After heaving a big sigh I said, "I finally found myself and I love it!"

******

I woke up earlier than usual that morning. I was feeling nervous, jumpy, anxious. I knew if I ate a morsel of food I would throw up. There was no way in hell that I could eat my breakfast that morning.

Today was the day all of us in class were going to face a video camera. We had to speak for two minutes on a topic that we were passionate about. The speech would be followed by a question from the audience where the participant on stage would have a minute to answer.

It isn't everyday that you speak into a video camera, so I ensured I would dress up for the occasion. I got my smartest shirt and trousers out along with a jet black blazer. While wearing my tie, I kept re-assuring myself - '33% of nervousness is fine, Sanjay. There is nothing to worry about!' I was echoing what Mr Vaidyanathan said during class the previous day while delivering a session on stage fright and how to combat this fear.

I walked out of my bedroom to where mom greeted me, "You're looking smashing sweetheart! You're going to do great." I smiled.

On reaching the venue, I found all my classmates in their best clothes, rehearsing their speeches. I looked into the mirror and did the same. I chose to speak on the situation in Kashmir and how there was a high need of dialogue to resolve the issue. Grandma having been a teacher on political science at one point in time, I had heard several stories from her around the Kashmir issue and so was extremely passionate about the subject. I really did feel it was high time the war ended and wished that this beautiful part of our country enjoyed peace again.

It was finally my turn to go on stage, wiping my damp hands against my trousers I walked up to the podium and looked straight into the camera. I spoke with passion and confidence for two whole minutes. I remember my speech ending with a standing ovation. I was pleasantly surprised by the appreciation I received from the audience. This was followed by a question from one of the members in the audience.

A young lady in a pink sari asked me "Do you think Jawaharlal Nehru is to blame for the Kashmir issue in the first place?" With grandma's inputs over the years on the issue I was able to tackle the controversial question with a politically correct answer that satisfied the questioner.

Standing in a corner, Mr Vaidyanathan caught my eye. I knew he was elated by my transformation.

Each of our speeches caught on tape were played back to us the following day. We were supposed to review each other's performance and rate each speaker on a three point scale - good, very good and excellent. Mr. Vaidyanathan made sure nobody received negative feedback. His class was about promoting optimism and feeling good after all. I was the only student in the class that received a unanimous 'excellent' from the rest of the class.

I was extremely satisfied with my performance on stage facing a camera. I suddenly felt public speaking was my calling. I went on to participate and win several intra-collegiate elocution competitions in the years to come.

******

Today was going to be an emotional day for me. It was the last day of my public speaking class.

As soon as I entered, I saw all my classmates gathered around the snacks table making a weekend plan to Alibaug. "Sanjay!" Dharmesh hollered to me, "You're coming right? We've already included you in the list of people coming anyway." I smiled and nodded indicating I would be coming. It felt good to be wanted for a change. I also think the change in my attitude towards myself made me look at everything around me more positively.

I sat down when Mr Vaidyanathan was about to begin. While he spoke, I looked, awe-struck at the man who changed my life, wondering how long this new attitude would last without him actually being around. There were a few minutes for class to end when Mr. Vaidyanathan picked up a piece of chalk to write on the board. That was the first time during the 7 day course that he used the board behind him to write something on it. He chalked down his email address and hand phone number and said, "All the best! Be happy and live life with optimism!"

After class, I walked up to him, touched his feet, hugged him, looked him in the eye and said, "Thank you sir! Thank you so much!" Mr Vaidyanathan smiled back and said, "Don't worry Sanjay; you will survive without me being there. You're stronger than you think you are." I was dumb founded. 'Is this man psychic? How did he know?' I thought to myself. Mr Vaidyanathan continued "Keep in touch, Sanjay!" But I never did. I thought of sir as an angel who did his job and was never to be touched or seen again.

While I walked out of that classroom, I turned around looking at the room in wonder one last time, knowing that I was leaving my past there in that very room never to run into it again.

On my way home, the kind of thoughts running in my head didn't surprise me anymore. 'I am fat. So what? I am asthmatic. So what? I have had failed friendships. So what? I have struggled with relationships at home. So what? I am slightly effeminate. So what? I am gay. So what? All that matters is what I have now. And I have the confidence in me being me. I am what I am. And that makes me happy. That train ride back home only re-assured me that I had come to terms with everything I had struggled with while growing up.

CHAPTER 6

Today I am 21 years old.

It was graduation day. My friends and I were thrilled in anticipation of wearing the graduation gown and receiving our degrees on a large stage in front of family and well-wishers. But to our disappointment, since there are thousands of students that graduate from Mumbai University every year, the norm was to collect degrees from the office counter.

Also, in case we wanted pictures of ourselves wearing the graduation gown, we had to pay a hundred bucks - 25 for renting the gown and 75 for a professional photographer to click and print the pictures. A hundred bucks was steep for students like us and we decided to pass on the pictures and splurge on eating out and celebrating instead.

We were at McDonalds and while munching on the burger Javed brought up the subject no one wanted to discuss, "So what plan does everybody have?" Saif put on his ignorant best, and throwing the ball back in Javed's court, asked, "In terms of what? Tonight?" Javed gave a sarcastic laugh and responded, "No, asshole! I'm not referring to tonight. I mean from here now where? We've graduated, what does everybody plan to do next?"

It was easiest for Rakhi to answer that question, everything was planned for her, "Me? I will go to fashion school starting June and after I graduate from there, the Armani's and Versace's of the world will want to hire me."

Saif had already started working in a call centre even before we had received our degrees, "Well I'm now at IXL. It's bringing in enough moolah. The job is easy. I think I'll continue here for a while till I find my calling." We absolutely knew what Javed was going to say post Saif's response; Javed and Saif were such good friends that they were inseparable. "Listen Saif, you told me there was a vacancy at IXL right? I'll interview there. You'll do something for me huh?"

Saif nodded confidently which translated as "Of course! Getting you a job is something my left hand could do!" I went next, "Well, I'm going to apply to some of the business schools for a post graduation degree. It seems logical since Rajiv did the same thing. He graduated from business school last year and landed a job with a hefty salary. Let's see how it goes." Joanna seemed the least focused amongst us at the time. "I don't know. I'm going home to see my parents for a bit. I'll chill for a few days and then decide."

I hated it when you're stuck in ironical situations like these. We didn't know whether it was right to celebrate or not. Like in this case, we finally did graduate so we definitely had the right to celebrate our success. But in the same breath we didn't know where the hell our lives were heading, so was it even right to have any kind of celebration in the first place?

Joanna's response to Javed's thought-provoking question triggered the realisation that all of us were absolutely directionless at the time (except for Rakhi). We knew that this would be a good time to kill the celebration before we officially termed ourselves as hopeless losers. While Javed, Saif and Rakhi got up to leave, Joanna and I decided to stay back for a bit and catch up on each other's lives.

"Even though I am clueless of what turn my life is going to take now, at least I find solace in the fact that I know you guys are here no matter what," I started the conversation.

"Well touché to that!" Joanna responded. "By the way I've been dating someone for a few weeks now...."

"What?" I felt unexpectedly betrayed at that moment; my best friend of many years didn't even bother to mention that she was seeing somebody. "How did this happen out of the blue? Why didn't you tell me?"

"Sanjay, I wanted to tell you. But he was insisting I kept it discreet for a while. And he still doesn't know I'm telling you this. You remember Dhruv Kapadia right?"

"That tall lanky guy? Are you serious?"

"Yes. I am 100% serious. And I need you to be fine with this. You know how important you are to me?"

I held her hand to comfort her, "Of course I'm fine with this. If you're happy, I'm happy." Joanna and I had now reached that stage in our friendship where we could almost read each other's minds. "Really, the last thing you should be bothered about is that he is a Hindu and you are a Christian. Let the relationship between the both of you build, you'll eventually know if this is right for you or not. Take it as it comes."

Joanna was glad she had my stamp of approval on her relationship with Dhruv. She smiled. The relief on her face was evident.

"You tell me... What is the latest with you?" she asked now chirpily.

"There is something I've wanted to tell you. I didn't tell you earlier because I got comfortable with it myself only recently." I said

My serious tone scared Joanna. "What happened? What is it?" She asked, concerned

"Please Joanna; promise me you won't stop talking to me because of this. I want you to know I am the same person, nothing changes because of this."

"Just tell me Sanjay, you're really scaring me now."

"I'm gay!" That was quick, spontaneous and unplanned. Just the way I had not anticipated it to be. Joanna was the first person I came out of the closet to and oh boy, didn't it feel good! It felt like a huge boulder was taken off my chest and thrown into the sea.

Joanna didn't believe me at first. But when she finally did, I saw a tear roll down her cheek. She didn't speak to me for two whole days. She finally called me on the third day after my coming out to her. She did all the talking, she didn't let me speak. "I'm sorry about the way I reacted. You know how important you are to me and this came as a complete shock. I didn't stop talking to you because you are gay but I knew that if I did talk to you I would break down. And I didn't want to put you in an uncomfortable spot. I felt sorry because my best friend had to be gay in a society like ours where it is condemned and not accepted. I feel bad that my best friend has to lead a tough life for no fault of his own. Are you sure this is the road you want to go down?"

I finally spoke. "Joanna, it took me years to finally accept it. There is no looking back now. The last thing I want is sympathy from you. I want you to treat me the way you always have treated me. You're important to me and I just thought that it is your right to know. I'm not the most comfortable about my sexuality yet but I know I'm getting there. It is just a matter of time."

Joanna then said, "Sanjay, if that makes you happy, it makes me happy. I will always love you no matter what."

"Love you too, Joanna."

******

'This page cannot be displayed' showed on the screen of my personal computer for the umpteenth time. I was trying unsuccessfully to log in to the website of one of the business schools I had applied to. I had applied to exactly 20 business schools that year and was unsuccessful in making it to 19 of them. I only had one more school to hear from and it was that very school's website I was continuously trying to log into. The results of the admission test were to be displayed online today. After a zillion attempts, finally the web page on the monitor screen displayed, 'Please enter your registration number here.' This was a 'Make or Break' moment for me. I carefully keyed in my registration number, crossed my fingers, said a little prayer in my head and waited for the result to display. What I feared most happened - 'I am sorry. You have not been short-listed. We look forward to you applying next year.' More than disheartened I was now anxious; the reaction from my parents is what I was not looking forward to.

I logged off from my personal computer and walked into the room where mom and Rajiv were seated. Reading my edgy face, Rajiv asked me, "What happened?"

Trying to sound as upset as possible so I could garner mom's sympathy, I responded to Rajiv's question. "I didn't make it to the last school as well."

However to my dismay, mom was not the least bit sympathetic. Mom had already begun showing menopausal tendencies in the recent past and I knew this was ideally not the best time to share any kind of bad news with her. In the most hyper tone I've ever heard mom take, she began rambling. "Oh no! What are you going to do now? This is going to be a complete waste of a year. Rajiv made it to one of the best business schools in the country right after graduation. That was absolutely the right path. *Hey Bhagwan! Isko thodi buddhi de de!* (Oh god! Give my son some intelligence!) Now, what are you going to do? Do you have anything in mind?"

While thinking - 'Thank god! Rajiv and I are on good terms now!' I looked to my brother for help. Rajiv picked up right on cue and began pacifying mom. "Mom, don't worry! Calm down. Sanjay can get a little bit of work experience before applying to business school again next year. This will even give him an edge over his classmates. Any kind of experience is always welcome in a business school. In fact, I'll check for a vacancy at the place I work, I'm sure we will find something for Sanjay."

Mom got even more hyper, "You keep quiet Rajiv! After you have met that girl Mahi you have been talking gibberish. What kind of job will he get with just a graduation degree?" Then looking in my direction, mom hollered, "You listen up! You start applying for jobs. And it better be something respectable. You are not going to be sitting at home doing nothing. And no call centres!"

After mom stormed out of the room, Rajiv and I exchanged a glance and began giggling. Patting me on my head, Rajiv said, "Don't worry bro! There is always next year! Go find something you want to do for now. I'll handle mom!" I smiled gratefully at my brother and went to pick up the newspaper to check for vacancies.

With the BPO boom in India, all the vacancies I saw were for call centre executives. My eye finally caught an advertisement in the corner of the page. It was by one of the leading search firms in the country - Search Jobs. Search Jobs had advertised a few vacancies on behalf of one of their clients. I spontaneously picked up the phone and called the number mentioned in the advertisement. "Good morning! This is Search Jobs! How may I help you?" I heard the voice on the other end of phone say.

I responded, "Good morning! My name is Sanjay. This was with reference to your advertisement in the paper today...."

With an increasing demand for call centre employees and a dearth of good candidates in the market (clearly supporting the basic fundamentals of demand and supply that I had learnt in Economics while at Graduation College), recruiters at search firms were always on the prowl for candidates like me.

The person at the other end of the phone (definitely a recruiter) cut me short. "Sanjay, you have called the right place. We have vacancies with some of the best companies in the business today. Telecom, financial services, travel - you name the sector, we provide you an opening with the best in that sector. I would suggest you meet me tomorrow so that we could get you a call centre job by the end of this week."

"You got me wrong. I do not want a job in a call centre," trying to sound as patient as I could.

"Then what do you want?" the recruiter responded evidently sounding pissed off.

"I want a job with Search Jobs. I want to be a recruiter." I had no clue what a recruiter did. All I knew was that I loved being around people because of the transformation I saw in me a few years ago and so I believed that Human Resources (HR) was my calling.

"A recruiter with us? Just send your profile across to me. I'll forward it to the appropriate person."

I did send in my CV and I did hear from the company a couple of days later. I interviewed and got the job. I was thrilled. I was to begin work the following Monday with a salary of Rs 6,000 a month.

******

Search Jobs was the place I met Dilnawaz Mistry aka Dilu. Dilu was a cute, bubbly, full of life, ditzy 22-year-old Parsi girl. Dilu and I were exclusive recruiters for the same client. As service providers to the same client, Dilu and I formed a strong professional and an even stronger personal bond.

"It's only chocolate liquor, chocolate plus liquor is definitely not equivalent to alcohol." Dilu said confidently handing over a glass to me at a hotel in Goa during an official getaway. "Look Dilu, you're 100% sure I will not get drunk with this stuff?" I interrogated. "I understand you don't drink alcohol. Trust me this is definitely not alcohol. You can't get drunk with this stuff." And with that re-assurance from Dilu, I gulped down a glass of chocolate liquor. "Wow!" I said aloud "This stuff tastes really good." "See, I told you it tastes just like chocolate." Dilu announced with a sense of accomplishment in her voice. After a few glasses of chocolate liquor, feeling a sense of elevation running in my head I progressed to having a few glasses of Vodka, again on Dilu's insistence. I began rambling after the second glass of vodka "Thanks Dilu! You really are a true friend. If it weren't for you I would have never had tasted the chocolate liquor." I knew I was drunk for sure when I began reciting the alphabets imitating a cartoon character on television.

In spite of tricking me into having alcohol, it was strange how I trusted Dilu so much that I came out to her within a year of knowing her.

"Are you sure you're gay? Are you sure you're not bisexual? Maybe you are into women as well? Have you had sex with a man? Did you enjoy it?" I was overwhelmed by the constant firing of questions by Dilu. But Dilu had a point there. I had met a few men on coffee dates (thanks to menforboys.com) but never did get physical with any of them. I knew I was attracted to them but how was I sure I would enjoy the intimacy with men when I hadn't actually gotten physical with any of them.

Taking from Dilu's unintended advice, I decided it was time to get physical with the next man I went out on a date with. I had a date for the following weekend and coincidentally my parents were out of town at the same time. I called Dilu before the date, "I'm meeting this guy Gautam today. Seems like a sweet chap." Dilu without wasting any time went straight to the point, "Don't get nervous Sanjay. Just go for it. Call him home and let him lead, you'll just follow and things will fall into place."

"But I'm really nervous about STDs." I said sounding worried.

"You're not going all the way on the first date. No anal sex, leave it at oral sex. And listen, you've heard of condoms right? I'm always for safe sex. And you better be too." Dilu said instructively. "It is my birthday today, so go make mamma proud. And fill me in, ok? I got to run now." Dilu hung up on me.

I met Gautam that night. He was a young muscular 19-year-old who had a steady girl friend. "This will be a no-strings-attached date." I remember him telling me. Gautam had a fetish for fat guys like me and so agreed to meet me for a casual encounter. As coached by Dilu, I called Gautam over and we did make out. We kissed, we caressed each other, we rubbed our bodies together, I also blew him. And man, did I love it! It felt like I was in heaven. After that, I was sure I did not need any other confirmation on my sexuality.

So, thanks to Dilnawaz Mistry, I was introduced to two vices - drinking and sex.

Today I am 24 years old.

"Put that knife down! What are you trying to do you maniac? Kill us?" Javed was yelling at Dhruv's sister. Joanna and Dhruv had been seeing each other for three years. It was today that their relationship ended.

A few days ago, my friends and I met up for dinner. "Man! I miss college. It's been ages since we have met up like this." Rakhi loudly voiced her sentiment at the dinner table. "Rakhi has a point there. We rarely meet up. We've gotten so busy with our lives" Saif continued supporting Rakhi's train of thought. "I hope we're still there for each other when a crisis hits us" I concluded.

Exactly three days later, my phone rang while I was at work. "Son, we need to see you urgently." It was Dhruv's dad on the other end of the phone. "What's wrong uncle?" I asked suspecting that there was something fishy. "We'll tell you when you're here."

I took the rest of the day off from work and rushed to Dhruv's house. I entered and took a seat on the couch in the living room. Dhruv's dad jumped straight to the point - "We heard about the Catholic girl!" he grumbled, staring at the ground. His tone sounded angry. I gulped, "Sorry uncle?" pretending not to hear the statement he had just made. Even louder, Dhruv's dad almost yelling, "I said we heard about the Catholic girl!"

"What about her?" I asked.

"Don't pretend son. We are aware that you know about their fling. And that is the reason that I have called you. We want you to tell them that they need to end this relationship."

Well such a reaction from Dhruv's parents was expected. Dhruv, a Hindu boy came from an affluent conservative business family. Joanna on the other hand, a Christian girl came from an upper middle class humble background.

I was scared by Dhruv's dad's tone; but I put up a brave face. "Uncle, I'm not going to tell them any such thing. They are two mature adults; they can make a decision on their own."

"I'm fine with my son screwing around but I'm not supportive of any marriage with a Catholic girl. Sanjay, you will tell them that they need to break up. Otherwise I will not have any option but to send some goons over to Joanna's place to teach her a lesson."

With disgust evident on my face, I said: "Hearing that from an educated man like you is appalling." I got up to leave.

"Listen Sanjay, speak to them or Joanna will see trouble."

I stormed out of the house. I called Joanna and told her to come over to my place. I informed Javed, Saif and Rakhi of the entire episode and told them to stand by for any kind of emergency.

Dhruv's dad called me repeatedly that day. "Have you advised that bitch to end the relationship with Dhruv? Tell me where does the slut stay? I will have goons sent over to her place; I have contacts; this is not going to be tough for me at all. It is best that you do as you are told. I will make that tramp leave the city." The continuous calls began to frighten me. I knew from the tone of his voice that he wasn't kidding.

After hanging up the phone on Dhruv's dad, I walked into the room where Joanna was sitting. I tried my best to hide my fear so that it did not influence her decision. She saw me wipe the brow of my forehead before I sat next to her. She looked at me and said, "Sanjay! I'm really scared!" She broke down and hugged me. I tried to pacify her, "It will be fine Joanna. Don't worry."

Joanna always came across as this fearless tigress that never cried. That was the first time since I have known her that I saw her cry. The last and only time she did cry was at her first cousin's funeral. "What do you want to do?" I asked her. "What do you think?" She asked me back. I decided to be honest. "It is getting too messy Joanna. I think you should end it. It's not worth all of this. And where is Dhruv in all this? Why isn't he stopping his dad from calling us and hounding us? I'm worried about your security more than anything else. But at the end of the day it is your call and I will support you no matter what." Joanna was still sobbing; she nodded her head and said, "I'll end it." Just then the phone rang. It was Dhruv's dad again.

"She has agreed to break up with Dhruv. Where should she meet him?" I told him

"Good job, Sanjay. Tell her to meet Dhruv at the promenade at 8 pm."

Immediately after hanging up I called up Javed, Saif and Rakhi and asked them to meet Joanna and me at the promenade a little before 8.

The five of us had never been that quiet. We just waited patiently at the promenade. Nobody said anything. We recognized the car that approached us. It was Dhruv's. Dhruv walked towards us. Strangely, we saw his mother and sister follow. Dhruv did not even have the courage to look us in the eye. He knew what a coward he had been the entire time. "Joanna, I don't think this is going to work." He said staring at the ground. Joanna could do nothing but just look at the man she had loved and sacrificed so much for in absolute shock.

"There, it is over now! You bitch, you're not coming anywhere near my innocent son. I know how you middle class girls trick rich boys like my Dhruv." Dhruv's mom said in a condescending tone.

"Mind your language, aunty." I said

"What language are you talking about? This slut slept in my mother's bed." Dhruv's sister yelled. She then removed a knife from her pocket and threateningly pointed it in our direction.

"Put that knife down! What are you trying to do you maniac? Kill us?" Javed yelled.

While this entire drama was on, Dhruv remained a silent observer. Rakhi knew that the drama was too much for Joanna to handle. She took her away. While Javed, Saif and I continued yelling at Dhruv's sister, Dhruv's mom tugged at his shirt indicating that it was time for them to go home. Dhruv sat in the driver's seat of the car and drove off with his mom and sister in tow.

After they left, we walked towards Rakhi and Joanna. Sitting on a bench all of us stared in the direction of the sea. After 20 minutes of absolute calm, Rakhi broke the silence saying, "You know what? Even though all of us are so busy with our own lives, I'm glad that at least we know we're still there for each other when a crisis hits us." Remembering our conversation over dinner a few days ago, we looked at each other and smiled.

******

It had been close to three years since I had begun working; but the pressure of enrolling in a business school never ended for me. "Sanjay, are you ever going to study further?" "I don't think Sanjay will ever pursue his masters." "Look at your brother Rajiv, so hardworking and diligent, why don't you do an MBA like him?" "Your career is not going to go anywhere without a masters degree." These were the kind of questions and remarks I was continuously subject to at any family gathering for many years since I had started working.

Since I knew Human Resources was my calling professionally, I only continued applying to schools that specialised in the subject. This was my third attempt at the entrance test to secure admission into the well renowned Tata Institute of Social Sciences (TISS). The Tata Institute of Social Sciences was one of the best schools in Asia for those students who aspired to become HR professionals. It was the first time in three years that I was called for an interview by the Institute after appearing for their aptitude test. I also had to cut short a professional trip to Sydney just to make it back home in time for the interview.

It was finally time for the results of the admission process to be announced. They were being displayed online and I had mentally prepared myself to see the usual apologetic statement that read - "I am sorry. You have been unsuccessful." I had already garnered an alibi in my head to take home to my parents for not making it to TISS. I wasn't being pessimistic; I was only being a realist. What were the odds of being one among 40 short listed students out of a total of over 7,000 applicants?

I guess god was in a generous mood that day. I was sure he was looking down on me and saying, "This loser has already seen a lot of shit in life, let's give him a shot this once." I downloaded the list of selected students and scrolled down the list of 40 names to spot a familiar name against serial number 17. It read Sanjay Sanghavi. With a wide gape I continued staring at the screen in disbelief.

If you've ever heard of the saying 'Try, try and try until you succeed!' in your moral science class, I really felt like the epitome of the statement at the time.

My academic year at TISS was to start in four weeks.

******

"Hi!" I greeted the girl sitting to my right on the couch I had occupied in the waiting area of TISS. "I'm Sanjay! Sanjay Sanghavi! First year - Human Resources." I introduced myself. "Hi!" she smiled back, "I'm Sonali Bhargava! Same as you, First Year - Human Resources." I looked at my future classmate and smiled. Sonali was a pretty dusky girl with sharp features. Her smile seemed infectious at the time. "So, we're going to be classmates for the next two years." I said, not knowing what else to say. Being the only two students who resided more than just a few kilometers away from the campus, Sonali and I had come in earlier then required. We had an hour to kill before the actual orientation. We chatted away till our conversation was interrupted by an unfamiliar voice, "You students can head towards the conference hall for the orientation. It begins in five minutes." It was one of the professors rounding up students to head towards the event.

Sonali and I walked in to the conference hall only to see most of the seats occupied. We noticed vacant seats at two different ends of the room and went to occupy them. A few minutes after we sat down, a short bald man in his early 50s walked in. It was the director of the institute - Dr. Vaidya.

Dr. Vaidya began his opening speech, "First of all it is our absolute pleasure to welcome all of you to the Tata Institute of Social Sciences. Look around you. You are all students from different fields - Social Work, Human Resources, Health, Development Studies. At the end of these 2 years, each one of you, having attained a degree in a different area of expertise, is expected to work together to lead our country to progress and development." Dr. Vaidya continued his dialogue stressing on how it was important for us to be over achievers using the path of integrity without hindering society or the environment around us.

Dr. Vaidya concluded his speech with a word of caution that left a particularly strong impact on me. "I would like to also emphasise that there will be no discrimination on this campus. Any kind of discrimination on the basis of caste, creed, religion or sexual orientation will be dealt with strictly here. You will be asked to pack your bags and leave." And with that statement, I suddenly felt secure. I felt liberated. That statement only reassured me that I made the right decision to quit a secure job and pursue this course at TISS.

******

"You don't make friends at B-School, you only make acquaintances," my brother was giving me a doze of *gyaan* the night before my second day at TISS. Rajiv had such a strong sentiment because he had had a bitter experience with his 'friends' when he was pursuing his post graduation. And so, like any older brother, Rajiv was providing his younger brother advice. He asked me to stay cautious and have no expectations.

In spite of Rajiv's advice, I was able to meet Riya Bakshi and Kritika Dayal. Both Riya and Kritika were similar in so many ways. Both of them were gorgeous, intelligent and mature. They would be termed as people who had it all. Riya and Kritika were similar in so many ways that they were often mistaken as twins.

It had been two months since the course started. Riya, Kritika and I were relaxing in their apartment, joking about the professor that taught us financial management. Kritika was a really good impressionist and mimicked professor Singh, "You kids of today! No focus at all! You bloody nincompoops!" After we rolled in laughter, there was a brief silence. Seizing the opportunity, I looked at the both of them still catching on their breath after laughing so hard and said, "By the way guys, I'm gay." Without any shock or bewilderment on her face, Riya responded, "We already knew that." I hadn't even realised that I had become so comfortable with my sexuality that it had now become apparent to the people around me. "Listen Sanjay, that doesn't make a difference to us at all. You don't need to justify your sexuality to us. We love you anyway!" Kritika added. I smiled at my friends. What followed was an intense discussion around hot guys and our respective tastes in men.

"So how do you meet guys?" Riya asked inquisitively.

"Well an online networking website is the best medium to use. Or else we have private parties." I responded

"You'll have parties? In Mumbai?" Kritika asked seeming absolutely shocked.

"Yeah, we do! But I've never been to one of them."

"Can we log on to the website and check out guys for you?" Riya asked me.

I didn't think twice. I picked up the laptop and typed www.menforboys.com in the web browser. Riya and Kritika cuddled up on either side of me and giggled while I logged in. They scrutinized each profile on the website and short listed a few for me to message. While we giggled and laughed, I looked at them both and began pondering on my brother's statement - 'You don't make friends at B-school, you only make acquaintances.' I smiled in my head, thinking 'I'm so glad Rajiv was wrong.'

******

I began to gather that good looks, a fit body and being well groomed were primary factors for any guy to fetch a date in the gay community. Thanks to me being overweight, my message inbox on the networking website behaved as if it had been hit by a drought. Even if I did happen to meet any guy for a coffee, the date always ended with the clichéd statement - "You're a really sweet guy. But....." I knew he didn't have to say anything further. Thank god my self-esteem was in place, I didn't know how else I would have survived so many rejections.

Kritika being a psychology major before she actually started her course at TISS became my regular counsellor. "Sanjay, what matters is what is within. Who cares about these superficial freaks! I'm sure this is all a build up for someone great to come along in your life. And trust me, when that happens it will be for good. And always look at where you were and what you have come to. You're sweet, charming, intelligent and also pursuing your masters from one of the best institutes in the continent. You're a catch, if anyone is. So please stop worrying."

Kritika's words of appreciation for me always helped when I was down. The fact that I had a counsellor in a friend at bay all the time definitely helped me not reach the stage of insanity.

Even though I had not hit it off with a lot of people physically, I was able to make two very close friends from the gay community. Vikram and Arth were two extreme ends of a spectrum. On one hand, Vikram was a hard core party animal, never believed in commitments and only indulged in no-strings-attached fun; Arth, on the other hand, was a sucker for love, hated the gay party scene and only indulged in sex with men after the third date.

"Please, there is no such concept as love in this community." Vikram initiated the conversation.

"You've never experienced it, that's the reason you're so negative. You won't even know what hit you when you fall in love." Arth retaliated to Vikram's negative comment.

"How long were you with your ex-boyfriend?"

"Two years...."

"Then what happened? You fell out of love?"

While Vikram and Arth continued having this debate around the concept of love, I remained quiet, gazing at the two of them. 'My god! These guys are so fit! No wonder they get the boys.' I thought to myself. I knew it was time to take my fate into my own hands. I either had the option to stay fat or get fit.

"I'm going to join a gym." I said interrupting the intense debate.

"What?" Vikram turned to me

"That is awesome! You should." Arth responded.

Since I was a little apprehensive of joining the gym alone, it took me a couple of days to convince Rakhi and Javed to join the gym with me. Finally, the negotiator in me successfully persuaded them and the three of us did join the local gym registering as members for the entire year.

CHAPTER 8

Today I am 25 years old.

It had been 14 months since I had begun exercising. I knew I had lost weight but just didn't know how much.

Riya and Kritika decided to take me shopping that evening. "Listen! Your clothes aren't doing anything for you." Kritika started the conversation. "Yeah, I agree. I mean you've lost all the weight, now these assholes online need to notice that. We got to go shopping." Riya continued. Kritika ended the conversation, "We'll meet you at the shopping mall at 6 this evening."

On my way home from the institute, I thought this would be a good time to get myself a complete makeover. I remember Dilu mentioned her friend Kelly was a stylist with one of the up market salons. I immediately called up the salon and fixed an appointment with Kelly.

"Have you ever used any hair product?" Kelly interrogated

"Never! I thought you lose hair with a hair product?" I asked with reference to the myth I had heard.

"That's utter rubbish. As long as you don't touch the product to the scalp it is fine."

Since the hair cut was still in progress, looking into the mirror I still couldn't figure out what the end result of the cut was going to finally be. Kelly then came back with the product. She took some of the gel in her hand and began running her fingers through my hair. "Look, you can either wear your hair to the side or you can spike it up like this or my recommendation is the messy look like this." The three different styles in a span of less than 30 seconds amazed me. I thought to myself, 'You can do so much with hair?'

My hair looked great. I never thought it could look like that! In excitement, I hugged Kelly, thanked her and rushed to reach the mall in time. Without doubt, Kelly became my regular stylist and a dear friend.

As soon as I reached the mall, Kritika and Riya were window shopping outside the lingerie store. As soon as I walked up to them, Riya exclaimed, "Oh my god! Your hair cut is awesome!" Kritika agreed with Riya and hugged me. "Why are we waiting here? Let's go shopping." I said excitedly.

It had been months since I had shopped. I used to always hate shopping because I never got styles or options in my size. "For the 42 inch waist jeans, we only have the casual fit; we don't offer any other styles." "I'm sorry this is the only colour available in your size." "I regret sir; we don't have that size available in our store." This was all I got to hear from mall attendants whenever I did gather the courage to go out shopping.

We were at the section that sold jeans. "Let's first get your size right. And then you can select from different styles - Low rise, boot cut, tight flair, skinny fit and the casual fit. We have a variety of colours too." The attendant said handing over a pair of jeans to me. "Sir, try this on."

I walked in to the changing room and looked at the tag that displayed the waist size. It read, "30 inch waist" I rolled my eyes with surprise and thought to myself, 'This is never going to fit me.' I was being a realist again. After being employed, my waist size did reduce from 44 inches to 42 inches without any exercise, but reducing from 42 inches to 30 inches in a span of 14 months seemed over ambitious to me. There wasn't any harm in trying, so I pulled down the pants I was wearing and attempted to try on the pair of jeans the attendant had handed over to me. The jeans surprisingly came on with ease and before I actually buttoned up, I looked towards the direction of the sky and said, "Please god!" Without any struggle or effort, I buttoned up. I looked into the mirror with complete shock. I kept staring at myself for a couple of minutes before I was snapped out of my day dreaming by Riya's voice, "Sanjay, you coming out or not?" I stepped out of the changing room and yelled "It fits!" "Congratulations!" said Kritika and Riya smiling warmly at me.

******

Logging on to www.menforboys.com had become a part of my daily routine. As soon as I logged in I received an alert which read as 'Your inbox is full. Please delete a few messages immediately.' It had been a week since I had uploaded pictures of my new look online; I was quite overwhelmed by the response I was receiving.

I had mixed reactions while reading through the messages. I smiled reading a few, I laughed reading others and I was plain disgusted reading the rest. "Hey hot stuff, wanna catch up for some hot action?" "Coffee sometime?" "I would love to fuck you so bad!" "I think I'm in love with you!" "Do you want to be my friend?" Out of the many messages I had read, I saved exactly seven of them.

So many shortlists at one go was completely new to me. So, I decided to call Vikram for advice on how to multi-task. I was sure that I couldn't call Arth for advice, because clearly the advice that I expected from Arth was not going to suit my needs. I was just looking for frivolous no-strings-attached sex.

Vikram was as cool as a cucumber while giving advice. He had the tips rolling out so quickly he could have written a book. "Sweetheart," he began, "Seven guys is not a big deal. First of all, every guy you meet, the contact number of the guy needs to be given to Arth or me before the date. Just in case you go missing the next day. When you meet, you first get together in a crowded place. You can never trust some of these gay bashers; they'll stoop to any level to hunt down and beat up gay men. If you're going to his place and you have the slightest doubt in your mind that this doesn't seem right, just get out of there. Trust your sixth sense like you would trust your mother. And lastly, always use a condom. Got it? You have my blessings, now go have fun!"

And with that advice my 'sexcapades' with seven different men began.

I think with these seven men, I met them all. Great kissers, bad kissers, terrible kissers, small sized, medium sized, large sized, foreplay lovers, foreplay haters, inexperienced, vanilla, kinky, muscled jocks, average executives, out of shape businessmen. Like I mentioned, I really had met them all.

Kelly and I were having an intense discussion on major turn offs in bed over a cup of coffee. "You know what I hate the most!" Kelly initiated her list of turn offs. It was obvious from her tone, that she was about to mention made her angry, very angry. "I hate it when you have to give instructions in bed! Some of these men just never get it right.... Such a turn off! Making out with me isn't a class right! You better know what you're doing!" "Oh my god, Kelly! You've actually given instructions in bed." I laughed in response. "I am so sure I will never bump into a nincompoop like that!" I mused.

The first guy I met was a tall, broad shouldered, muscular cruise line steward. He looked great but could not hold a conversation without the word sex for more than 30 seconds. He could definitely be termed as the world's worst kisser. "Why are you biting me? Can you please kiss with your mouth open? And do not use your teeth while kissing." It felt really weird giving instructions when you were involved in something as intimate as foreplay. Now I knew exactly what Kelly meant in our conversation a few weeks ago. As soon as he bit my nipple hard, I knew I had to end it. "You're hurting me! Get off me!" I yelled. I picked up his clothes, handed them over to him and asked him to leave. I had no time to waste; I had six more to go.

It was our Diwali break in college. Saumil's parents were visiting Shirdi for the weekend. Seizing the opportunity, Saumil, Javed, Saif and I decided to have a night out at his place. We rented out an X-rated movie *Menina Inocente! Menina Impertinente*! After a bit of an online investigation, Saif found out that the movie was made in Brazil and the title translated from Portuguese as 'Innocent Girl! Naughty Girl!' The entire time we watched the movie, my eyes were glued to the Brazilian lead actor. He was tanned, muscular and had the largest endowment I had ever seen. He kissed, caressed and made love to the lead actress so passionately. I didn't even have to stroke myself; I had an orgasm just looking at him move.

Recalling the lead actor from *Menina Inocente! Menina Impertinente!* I was obviously excited to meet Pedro an expatriate who was in India for a short term assignment. He hailed from Brazil and spoke with the cutest accent. "*Olá Sanjay!! É realmente um prazer encontrá-lo!*" (Hello Sanjay! It really is a pleasure to meet you!) He greeted me with a peck on the cheek. I felt like he was singing to me in that accent, so melodic, so beautiful. We went for a movie and while we stepped out of the cinema hall, he looked towards me with the dreamiest stare and asked me, "Would you like to come home for some coffee?" With those eyes and that accent did I have a choice? Without even thinking twice, I nodded my head and said, "Of course!" Pedro was a giver in bed and boy did he know how to use those lips. He began kissing me on my forehead, moved down to my eyes, to my nose, to my lips. He kissed every part of my body to complete perfection. He caressed my thigh, my stomach, my butt while he kissed me. He did everything for me; I didn't have to move a muscle. I only had to move the muscles in my tongue while kissing him and while giving him a blowjob. Fortunately, just like the lead actor in the X-rated movie, Pedro didn't disappoint me. I, however, never had the courage to meet Pedro again, I knew if I had sex with him one more time I would fall in love with him. And the agenda on my mind with these seven men was clearly no-strings-attached fun.

I was reading the spring issue of Cosmopolitan where starlets were talking about their sexual fantasies. It made an interesting read. I began thinking of my own. My fantasy? I thought hard. Ahhhh yes..... Having sex with a straight man! I'm so sure that would be the best sex I ever have!

Next in queue in my 'sexcapades' was a 30-year-old businessman. I decided to meet our man after a long day at college which included a lecture on a Group Dynamics concept called Power. I was pooped and frustrated and clearly wanted to hold the power quotient in tonight's encounter. "Why aren't you kissing me?" I questioned him. "Why am I not satisfying you without the kissing?" he questioned back. "I'm the one blowing you, you aren't doing anything." I reacted to his absurd come back to my question. From the tone of my voice, he knew I wasn't just going to sit there and do all the work myself. He responded, "I have a confession to make. I'm actually straight. I'm just too tired to jerk off myself, that's the reason I called you, so you could do it for me." "What?!" I yelled. I was so upset; I left the act mid way and got up to leave. I put on my clothes and just before I was about to step out of the door to his apartment, I slapped him across his face and said, "I'm not a whore, you son of a bitch! Go get yourself a hooker." I slammed the door on my way out. My fantasy? I'll need to think about it. Nope, I'm having sex with no straight men no more.

During 'project sexcapades' I had sex in a movie hall, in a car, at a gay party and in my parent's bedroom. However, the last of these marathon sexual encounters triggered something completely unexpected.

"So how are the seven men, sweetheart? Fallen in love yet?" Vikram asked me on the phone while I was getting ready for my date. "I'm meeting the seventh tonight. I love no-strings-attached fun! I can do this all the time. I don't understand this gibberish called love anymore." I laughed hysterically in response to Vikram's question. "You little bitch! Go enjoy yourself!"

Last, I met Farhan Azmi. Farhan was an average looking rich south Mumbai brat who only had his *chaat* (Popular Mumbai street food) at five star hotels. While we were out on a drive in his car, it didn't matter whether his car was in motion or not, we made out like two wild animals in an urban jungle. "I really want to see more of you." Farhan mentioned before dropping me back home. "Sweety, I'm sorry my parents are home. You can't see more of me. You've seen enough." I responded. With large puppy eyes, almost begging, he said "Please baby! I really want to see more of you." I knew my hormones were taking over me. I looked at the dimly lit staircase of the building I stayed at and said to him, "Go park the car and come with me." I did have sex that night, in the dimly lit stair case right outside my apartment door while my parents were inside sleeping. After we were done, Farhan bid me goodbye. I walked into my bedroom and switched on the light. Looking at myself in the mirror, I started crying. 'What happened to you Sanjay? Why have you become this slut?' I thought to myself. I thought I was enjoying this but I was clearly disgusted by what I had done in the past few days. I really didn't know what triggered this reaction but knew I had had enough of this frivolous sex. It was satirical how this guilt trip I subjected myself to seemed planned right after the seventh and last sexcapade. I knew I had to take the same path Arth was taking. I have and always will be a believer in love. I was now looking for a meaningful relationship.

******

It didn't take me long to bump into Swapnil Kulkarni. Swapnil was a 31 year old, tall, ambitious, driven individual. I knew this was the kind of man I would want to settle down with right after my first conversation with him on the phone. Swapnil said all the right things, had the same thoughts and views as I did, respected me for who I was and was vocal about the possibility of us being together whenever we did finally decide to meet in person.

Our busy schedules and travel plans did not allow us to meet for the next eight days. We continued chatting on the phone for all those days and our relationship only grew stronger. It was weird how I was beginning to fall in love with a person I had not even met.

"Swapnil, we really need to slow down. We haven't

even met yet." I was worried while speaking to Swapnil the night I was in Delhi for an intra-collegiate competition.

"Baby, really there is nothing to worry about. We've seen pictures; we've been speaking every day. What could be so drastically different when we meet in person?" Swapnil responded trying to calm me down.

We finally did meet in person. I knew that this was it for me. The phone conversations were enough for me to know that this was the man I wanted to spend the rest of my life with. Unfortunately, it wasn't the same for Swapnil.

After meeting me, he began avoiding my calls. He finally called the following morning. I was in class and had to excuse myself from the lecture to take his call. "Why haven't you been answering my calls, Swapnil?" I screamed. "Listen Sanjay! I've been thinking about us. This isn't going to work out. I just didn't feel the connection after we met yesterday. You're way too young for me. You're like a younger brother to me." Swapnil responded. "A younger brother?" I bawled like a baby. I hung up the phone on him and didn't go back to class.

Thankfully, Riya had missed the morning lecture and so I headed towards the girls' apartment. As soon as I entered, I began crying and hugged Riya. "What's wrong, sweetheart?" She asked me sounding worried. I narrated the entire incident to her. "What a bastard! Let him go to hell. You deserve better. This will pass Sanjay and you're stronger than that."

After catching up on some sleep at the apartment, I woke up and grabbed Riya's laptop. I logged in to my email account and began writing an email to Swapnil.

Swapnil,

Hoping this email comes to you as a pleasant surprise. After this morning's conversation I had to pen my thoughts down on email so that I could feel better.

Well, obviously I was upset after the conversation and hence the water works. But trust me I will be fine, so you don't have to worry at all.

I also wanted to write this email to thank you for the most amazing eight days of my life. I never thought I would find a like-minded guy but I did. You have definitely given me hope that there are nice guys among gays who have similar views on commitment like I did. It's amazing how we connected on so many levels.

These eight days have been phenomenal. From you, I received the kind of attention I've never got as a child or an adolescent. I have never spoken to such a genuine, nice person from the community and you were an absolute pleasure to talk to. I loved the constant messages, I loved the late night conversations, I loved the way you complimented me and I loved the way you called me 'baby'. You gave me a new ray of hope.

And now, I'm going to miss all of this.

Well, it has only been eight days so I am hoping to come out of this soon. It does seem kind of weird though, that I haven't picked up the phone to message you even once today.

I'm sorry to have disappointed you when we met in person. I am sure you had your expectations. Unfortunately mine were met and yours weren't. Well I guess the 'Sanjay' you wanted to see was in hiding that day.

I only pray for you to be happy. I hope you find someone who respects your view and understands where you're coming from. You deserve the best and I unfortunately wasn't the best for you. Whoever you ultimately end up with is going to be one helluva lucky guy!

Swapnil, I was beginning to fall in love with you and I am glad you snapped me out of it just in time. I don't think I will be strong enough to keep in touch with you as mere friends; I would rather go down as someone you were very fond of. And definitely not your younger brother.

Only wishing you the best in life.

Sanjay

The process of writing the entire email was painful but after completing it, I felt immense relief. I definitely loved Swapnil and knew for a fact that I may never meet a man like him or even fall in love again. But I felt proud that I took the step in bringing the vague relationship between the two of us to a closure. In spite of being dumped, I didn't feel like a loser at all. The Sanjay in his teens would have bawled for days and would have eventually picked up a blade and slit his throat. But that isn't the Sanjay I am today. Sanjay is all grown up, having gotten stronger, tougher, mature. I knew there were bigger challenges in life and I was ready to face those head on.

Swapnil never did reply to the email. But he did go down as the first man I ever truly loved.

******

After my relationship with Swapnil ended, I knew what I needed was a good old-fashioned drinking binge. I initiated the plan with the girls at their apartment.

After the initial rounds of vodka shots, Kritika decided to ramble first. "I've been in a relationship for eight fuck'n years. And out of those eight years, Rahul and I have actually been physically together for just one."

Kritika was in a long distance relationship with Rahul, her childhood sweetheart who moved to Australia a few months after they initiated a romance. They decided to give the romance a shot in spite of the distance and they had been together for eight years now.

Kritika continued rambling. "I hate the fact that I am here and he is there. I feel incomplete. It's so fuck'n tough. There are so many firsts that we still need to do together. Can you believe it? In these eight years we haven't been to an A-rated movie together, we haven't gone out for a night of clubbing together, we haven't even sat down to have a candle-light dinner together."

A tear rolled down her cheek while she spoke about Rahul. It seemed so easy being on the other side and saying, "It's just a long distance relationship; you'll get through this." But Kritika's story only made us realise how tough it would be to sustain seven out of eight years being away from each other. As an immediate reflex, Riya and I got up to hug her.

After a brief moment of silence, I yelled in a drunken voice, "Riya, you want to go next with your sob story?"

Riya always found it tough to open up. Six shots of

alcohol too didn't help. But the seventh one did the trick. "Well the love of my life - Ranveer is so sweet, so smart, so funny, so adorable, so loving. When I'm around he sees nothing but me. I love him so much. He is absolutely perfect. I really think so. But my family...nope...not my family. They think he isn't the one I should be with. There are supposedly better men for me. Come on I'm 23 for crying out loud! I think I'm mature enough to make that decision. At the same time, I love my family so much. I am so indebted to them."

Riya knew she was getting way too emotional. She immediately took a detour around where her conversation was heading. "But I guess I will cross the bridge when I get there. Right now I love being with my family. I love being with Ranveer. So the present is what really matters." It was so strange how someone could have such unnerving control over their emotions. Riya never cried. She knew exactly when the waterworks were going to begin and always took control before that first tear rolled out just in the nick of time.

This drinking session only brought the three of us closer. We identified something in common between us. We really did not have it all. We were all desperate when it came to our men.

Kritika was desperately looking out for the strength to sustain a long distance relationship with the man she loved so dearly; Riya was desperately looking out for acceptance from her family to marry the man she loved so dearly and I, I was desperately looking out for the courage to let go of the man I loved so dearly.

******

It had been two years since Rajiv got married and moved to Hong Kong with Mahi. It was this year on his annual visit back home that I decided to come out of the closet to him.

Coming out of the closet to my brother was going to be very tough on me. Rajiv meant the world to me. I was worried; it could sour our relationship. I would be devastated if that happened. But my brother had to know, being my confidant, my best friend, my mentor, my guide he really had the right to know.

The fear of Rajiv not accepting me for my sexuality was so overpowering that I decided to play it safe while coming out to him. I decided to tell Mahi first at my aunt's funeral.

Just as I had anticipated, Mahi was very supportive and understood exactly where my anxiety was coming from. "Don't worry Sanjay! I'll handle this. I'm sure Rajiv is going to understand. At the end of the day, it's not a choice you made; you're just born this way. The only choice you have made is to accept your sexuality and I'm so proud of you for that." I trusted Mahi and I'm glad I did.

The following day, I spoke to her on the phone.

"So, what did he say?" I asked curiously.

"Really Sanjay, he is going to be fine with it. Just tell him," Mahi responded.

"And how are you so sure about that?"

"I initiated the conversation telling Rajiv that I thought my cousin Karthik is gay. And I wasn't sure how I should react in case he decides to come out to me since we're so close."

"And what did Rajiv say?"

"He said that I should accept Karthik for who he is; whether he was straight or gay really didn't matter at the end of the day."

"But that is about Karthik. It is different when it comes to your own sibling."

"Sanjay, will you listen to me? My conversation with Rajiv isn't over yet."

"What happened then?"

"Rajiv then mentioned that he actually thinks you are gay too. But he never had the courage to ask you. He thought you may take offence to someone doubting your sexuality in case you really were straight."

"Really? Rajiv always thought I was gay?"

"I also asked him for his reaction in case you did decide to come out of the closet to him some day."

"What did he say? What did he say?" I knew the

answer to this question would finally give me the confidence to tell my brother of my true sexuality.

"He said, and I quote, 'Sanjay's sexuality does not determine my relationship with him. I love him whether he is straight or gay.' That is the reason I'm telling you to go ahead and tell Rajiv, he really is going to be fine with it."

I was thrilled. I was simultaneously surprised by my brother's potential reaction. I always thought Rajiv was homophobic. He always made fun of sitcoms like *'Will & Grace'*. He always hated me as a kid for being so effeminate and not being a 'real' boy.

I decided to finally come out to my brother. That night Rajiv and I were chatting in my bedroom till the wee hours of the morning. I narrated everything right from the bullying I was subject to in school to my issues with self-esteem to my hatred for him as a kid to my difficult times at home and school with me being suicidal for many years to my transformation at the public speaking class.

Rajiv was visibly upset by the narration, "How come I never knew this for so many years? I thought I had a strong contribution to what you are today - confident, strong, ambitious. And now I realise that I was actually a contributor to the shit you went through for so long. I'm so sorry Sanjay, I didn't know that. I hate myself for having done this to you."

I tried to calm my brother down, "Rajiv, I love you. You've more than covered up for all the crap in the past. I look up to you now. And you are without doubt a strong contributor to who I am today. Your advice has always worked for me. I thank god every single day for giving me a brother like you."

Rajiv smiled. We were quiet for a bit before I started talking again. "By the way, there was one more thing I struggled with while growing up." "What was that?" Rajiv asked me. Trying my best not to hold back, I responded "My sexuality. And now I know I'm definitely gay."

Rajiv's reaction was just as Mahi mentioned it - calm, composed, mature. "Sanjay, you're my brother, your sexuality doesn't make a difference to our relationship. I love you no matter what." Rajiv and I rarely hugged but that day we did. "Isn't it ironical how Mahi and I were just discussing this the other day?" Rajiv questioned smiling. There was no way in hell that I would tell my brother that I decided to come out to his wife before I came out to him. I strongly believe that there are good lies too; and I mentally decided that this was most definitely one of them.

Seeing the possessive older-brother side to Rajiv after I came out to him was amusing. He wanted to know all about the boys I was dating, where they came from, the kind of people I hung out with, all of it. What also followed were numerous lectures on 'safe sex'. All through his advice, I learned to smile patiently.

Today I am 26 years old.

"I do not understand the significance of the linkage of this particular system to performance management. It just doesn't make any sense." Sonali was being assertive while putting her point across to the group. "What is there to understand? From the system you short list competencies which are linked to the actual skills required for the job. In case you do not display these skills you are not a performer," a class-mate in the same group said trying to defend the group's ideology. "So how is a person's performance being measured on the basis of skills alone? Isn't that supposed to be linked to potential of the person and not performance?"

Sonali countered back strongly. I had never seen Sonali that assertive, the only side I had seen to Sonali was the timid sweet girl that I met on day one of the course. "Guys, I do think Sonali has a point here. I think it would be best that we come back with some more notes tomorrow. We could then finally end this debate and know where we are going." I intervened when I was convinced with Sonali's argument. It was close to 11:00 pm when we decided to depart.

"Thanks for backing me!" Sonali mentioned while we were walking out of the campus gate.

"Hey it was all you! You convinced me so I decided to back you." I replied. "But what happened to you? You seemed like a little tigress out there."

"Na! Not Really! I guess you sometimes need to scream

to make your presence felt. Or else you're ignored. I learnt it the hard way."

And that statement made me realise how different people had different takeaways from this school called TISS. TISS gave Sonali assertiveness, a new found confidence and an assurance to voice her opinion when she had to.

Standing at the campus gate, Sonali and I spoke for exactly one hour. It was so strange how between two individuals who were so detached from each other over the entire academic year; there was suddenly a connection, a connection that could in no way be explained.

"I knew you were a nice guy right from the time we spoke on day-one of the course. You were like my first friend on campus," Sonali said smiling at me. "By the way have you finalised on the NGO you're going to intern with?" She asked out of the blue.

At TISS, each student as part of the curriculum had to intern with a non-profit organisation for a month in order to be successfully eligible for the degree. In response to her question, I mentioned I would be interning with an organisation called Aradhana Trust that did work for the rights of the LGBT community.

"LGBT? You mean lesbians, gays, bisexuals and transgenders?"

"Yup! That's right! I am a homosexual; so I thought this would be a good opportunity for me to give back to the community."

"Hey that's great!"

"You should do your stint there too."

"Don't get me wrong! I'm all for gay rights, but I think I would be a little uncomfortable. I might get a bit spooked out."

Honestly, I was a little spooked out too. The thought of being around and working with the transgenders scared me a bit. My thoughts were coloured by what I had seen for all these years on television. My very reason for asking Sonali to join me for the internship at Aradhana was clearly out of my desire to have a support system while I interned.

But I had to do this for myself with or without Sonali. I guess there are some things in life that you have to do alone. And this was going to be one of those things.

Oh! And my takeaway from TISS? TISS gave me a new lease of freedom, the freedom to express myself and just be.

******

It was the first day of my internship at Aradhana Trust.

While I sat on a wooden chair, I looked around. I tried not to be distracted by the dark pink walls. The reception desk was occupied by a cute young man in his early 20's. Behind him was a poster that read, "Have safe sex! Always use a condom!" To my right was another poster explaining the difference between a homosexual, a transgender and a transvestite. While flipping through one of the magazines, I was intrigued by an article on Section 377 of the Indian Penal Code and how this particular act was being misused by police personnel to discriminate against homosexuals.

Suddenly a woman in a green sari sat next to me, "You don't mind if I sit here, do you?" She smiled. I smiled back only to realise I was sitting next to a transgender. Before the uneasiness showed on my face, I chided myself silently, "Sanjay, you are such a hypocrite! You expect people not to hold any kind of bias against you because you are gay and you yourself are being so judgmental about the person next to you. You really make me sick."

My train of thought was suddenly broken, "Are you Sanjay Sanghavi?" I looked in the direction of a man wearing a bright orange *kurta*. I nodded, "Yes."

"Hi! I'm Sumit. You'll be working with me. I had a look at your CV. It is quite impressive. There are lots you could do to help me and our organisation."

"I would love to be of some assistance around here. What can I do?" I responded excitedly.

"There are a couple of projects. We would like you to do a competency mapping exercise, have interview evaluation sheets ready for different roles and also design a performance management system for us. You tell us what interests you the most and you could contribute in that area."

"But these are all HR projects." I said sounding disappointed.

"Yes. What did you expect?"

"I was really keen to do some work in the area of gay rights. I mean awareness building, counselling or something of that sort." That vague response made me realise I had no clue what an LGBT organisation like Aradhana Trust did. I decided it was best to shut up and do the work that was assigned to me in the first place.

While I worked on my projects,I had the opportunity to interact with a lot of people from the community. One man that left a mark on me in particular was Shashikant Hegde.

"I was nine when I knew that there was something different about me." He began telling me his story. "My mother saw me trying on her *bindi* and *kajal* (accessories for women). She gave me the worst beating of my life. I knew I had to run away. I came to Mumbai. There is something so funny about this city. You love to hate it and you can't do anything but force yourself to love it. And my God the things people do to survive in this city."

"Why? What did you do?" I asked getting more and more curious about Shashikant's story.

"*Arre*, I joined the *hijra* (eunuch) community. I begged for alms during the day and played prostitute by night. Imagine losing your virginity at the tender age of ten. My anus bled every time I was fucked. And these mother fuck'n bastards didn't have a conscience at all. The assholes in fact enjoyed it when I bled. It seemed like an achievement to them, I guess they were trying to prove a point to their egoistic selves."

I felt a little sick in the stomach and barely managed to release a sigh and say, "That is terrible."

"But then Mr Shekhawat got me to Aradhana. I'm so thankful to him. This place really has changed my life for the good. I pray to god nobody else suffers like I did just because of being a transgender."

Looking at Shashikant's attire, he seemed like any regular Joe, "You're a transgender?" I asked surprised.

"Yeah! I am." Laughing off my astonished look, Shashikant continued, "My appearance? I'm only Sushmita when I walk out of the trust in the evenings. This look gives me the opportunity to reach out and work with more young kids like you. Or else I'm just termed as the freak."

"But you're sacrificing being you?" I spontaneously quizzed Shashikant.

"The sacrifice is completely worth it. Sanjay, you know we still live in a conservative society. I'm sure even you would be uncomfortable having a conversation with me if I wore a skirt." I looked away, clearly embarrassed by the truth. Shashikant continued, "And by being Shashikant I am able to do so much more for our community. There is more acceptance as Shashikant; people are willing to listen. Don't get me wrong here, I fight the same battle but with a voice that is listened to and not ridiculed at."

I looked at this man in awe. He was willing to give up his true self for a cause which did not necessarily have a happy ending. And this was not a cause he was fighting for himself alone. Shashikant had the choice to live as Sushmita and be true to himself but he sacrificed his happiness for a larger purpose, for a larger group of people.

I looked back at the years gone by and thought of the many times I was ridiculed and scoffed at for just being myself. I remembered the time I chose not to be true to my sexuality and picked the easy path of being a hypocrite. I reflected on the many times I laughed at homosexuals and transgenders just to disguise my true orientation. I relived the time I broke all barriers to finally accept my true self. And while I recapped my entire life gone by in exactly 60 seconds, I realised that the focus has always been on 'ME'. Shashikant, on the other hand, thought of everybody else but himself. I was gripped by a man so honest, so genuine, so selfless, so strong. I began introspecting on why transgenders left me jittery in the first place. Because I was influenced by a societal mindset that thinks these people aren't worthy of an existence and are a bad influence on the youth? I was so mistaken.... If anybody is worthy of setting the right example for the next generation, it is people like Shashikant. After all, he is a walking talking representation of values and principles that every parent wants inculcated in their children - strong-mindedness, integrity and selflessness. To me, Shashikant was a true inspiration.

After this chat with Shashikant, transgenders didn't leave me uncomfortable or edgy anymore. Looking at them now, I only feel a sense of admiration and the utmost respect for them. I realised transgenders make an extremely tough choice in life. Choosing the path of being themselves results in them only being ridiculed, mocked at and ostracised by most people. I definitely didn't want to be one of those people.

I decided to show my remorse for being a hypocrite when it came to transgenders for all these years. A day before my internship at Aradhana came to an end, I left a thank you card addressed to 'Sushmita'.

******

While I peered into my laptop, I was concentrating hard to make sense of the attrition data. Frustrated, I leaned back on my chair, threw my hands into the air and screamed, "This doesn't make any sense!" I shut the excel file I was working on and just as I was about to leave my work station to head towards the restroom, a voice hollered, "Kavya! Lovleen! Sanjay! Lunch guys?" I turned around to see it was my new boss - Ravi Gill.

It had been five months since I had started working with WSU Life, a leading life insurance company in the country post the completion of my masters from TISS. Ravi had only joined WSU Life as our boss a day before, from one of those multi-national banks that recently went bust. Kavya, Lovleen and I were all part of the same team. Our job was basically to provide HR support or as they refer to it these days, as people support to the Alternate Channels business at WSU.

Kavya was a young, aggressive, nice looking woman who hailed from the northern part of the country. And when I say aggressive, I mean aggressive. God save those business teams that did not abide by people policies, she could manage to kill with her eyes alone. I remember when one of the employees went up to her with a complaint against his manager. "I was hospitalised for 10 days and now she wants me to upload the leave against my available privilege leave and not my sick leave. I have receipts from the hospital too." He had said to Kavya. Kavya immediately called for the manager, stepped into the adjacent conference room with her and point blank asked, "What's the issue with Rohan's leave?" While the manager began justifying the entire episode with a business need, Kavya listened without saying a word. With her angry eyes, she stared, stared and continued to stare at the manager. The only time Kavya spoke during this entire episode was when she stepped out of the room, "Don't mess around with people issues Aditi. You'll never be a successful manager." The next day Aditi resigned.

Lovleen, on the other hand, was a pretty looking air-head. Lovleen only spoke of three things - her clothes, her shoes and her hair. "My god! You have to check out the sale at Dimpys, 75% off on Prada." She had screamed that morning as soon as she entered the office. It had been eight months since Lovleen had been with WSU. I wondered how she survived that long in the organisation. After a bit of introspection, however, I realised that all the businesses she provided support to were headed by men. "Lovleen! You really are a star! What would I do without you?" Once in every three days Arindam Bandopadhyay, head of the Broking unit walked into the area we sat in and hollered the statement. What was more annoying was Lovleen's standard response, "Oh Arindam! Stop embarrassing me now!" Being my cheeky self, one day I decided to ask Arindam, "What did Lovleen do? I'm really keen to know. I want to replicate the same for my business teams and get the kind of appreciation she gets." Arindam was at a loss for words. "Ummmm.... She walked the floor and engaged my team yesterday."

Arindam never came back to the HR bay to praise Lovleen again.

None of us were surprised when Ravi called us for lunch on his second day at WSU. Ravi was only following a norm. All new bosses are expected to bond with their team members over food and drinks. It is like what the butchers say, 'Stuff the sheep before you slaughter it!' Ravi was a good looking man in his early 30s. He was tall, had the body of a swimmer and was very well-groomed. Anybody's first impression of this man would be "Wow!" But my first impression of him was definitely not a lasting one.

Our conversation at lunch began with introductions - where we hailed from, business schools we graduated from, past experience, current roles. Ravi then decided to take the informal route and move away from the more conventional, formal topics. "So did everybody want to get into HR at this table? What did you actually want to be professionally?" 'Is that a trick question?' I thought to myself. I truly believed that a boss and a subordinate can never be friends and this belief forced me to always think twice before responding to my boss. 'Maybe he was trying to assess how focused we are about our careers.' I continued thinking. I also wanted to observe what my colleagues would say in response to his question. There was a brief silence at the table.

Thankfully I wasn't the only one thinking too much and I guess that made me feel sane. Ravi then tried to fill the uncomfortable silence at the table and responded to his own question, "Well I wanted to be a soccer player. I've played soccer in school and college representing my state. I play soccer over the weekends too." Lovleen, in an extremely flirtatious tone said, "Wow! Soccer! I love men who play soccer! You know, I wanted to be a writer." "Yeah! Her book will be called 'How to survive in an organisation? - A book for the brain-dead!'" Kavya whispered to me. I tried my best to hold back my laughter before Kavya spoke, "I would have been a social worker, I'm a feminist to the tee, I would have slaughtered all those men who beat their wives." Ravi then turned towards me and asked, "What about you Sanjay? What did you want to be? A belly dancer?" Ravi smirked and cracked up at his own joke. Kavya and I exchanged a look of astonishment, while Lovleen began giggling, picking her cue from Ravi's laugh. "Oh Ravi, you are so funny!" She exclaimed rubbing her palm against his shoulder. I chose to ignore the statement and said, "If I had the choice, I would have been a theatre actor. I love being on stage in front of an audience." After 45 minutes of arbitrary chat at the most mind-numbing lunch of my life, we were on our way back to the office.

Now since Ravi had fed us the food, it was time for the drinks. On the way to the office, Ravi initiated conversation, "Guys! Drinks on me tomorrow night!" I was now wondering when the slaughter would begin. Lovleen's reaction was as I expected, "That is so much fun! I'm going to change into my night club wear before I head to where you're taking us."

"Oh by the way," Ravi continued, "Your partners are invited too!" Then giving me the most condescending look he said, "Boyfriends too!" I smiled, and as soon as he turned his face away, I gave him the most snarling look behind his back that would put Catwoman to shame.

I never believed in screaming about my sexuality from the roof top. 'Why did anybody at work have to know?' I always thought. A heterosexual never proclaims that he or she is straight so why does a homosexual have to proclaim that he or she is gay. I always knew that there was speculation and gossip about my sexuality at work but had never had such an in-your-face experience as I had with my boss today. It was obvious from my boss' disdainful comments that he knew I was gay and was clearly uncomfortable with it.

Over the next couple of weeks, for the first time in my professional life, I not only see but experienced discrimination myself. You hear so much about discrimination at work for various reasons but actually being subject to it was a different story altogether. My boss stopped interacting with me, my job was reduced to almost doing nothing, my interactions with the business teams were kept minimal, I was left out of team meetings and I was asked to just do menial tasks.

Just the other day, Ravi called for a team meeting. As soon as I was about to enter the meeting room with a note pad in tow following Kavya and Lovleen, Ravi stopped me at the door and said, "Oh Sanjay, you aren't required for this meeting. Can you please make sure you hand over the data I had asked for by end of day?" "What data?" I questioned. He replied, "I needed data on the number of applicants for each position vacant." Surprised by the strange request, I further questioned, "What do you need that for?" "It is for some analysis I am doing. Could you do as you are told now?" That response made me feel like a heap of crap being squashed by a pair of military boots worn by my boss.

A few weeks later, I finally gathered some courage and decided to raise the issue with my boss. "Ravi, I need to talk to you."

"Not now, Sanjay, come back later"

"Can we block some time for this evening then?"

Ravi knew I was going to be persistent, "Fine, let's sit now."

In the meeting room, I confronted him. "I am twiddling my thumbs all day long. Every time I ask for work I'm given some menial task to do. I have no interactions with business. I am not part of any team meetings. What is going on?"

My boss' response disoriented me. In the most naïve tone he asked me, "Really? You have been feeling like that? I had no clue at all. I'm glad you brought this up."

What I didn't know was my boss had another strategy in mind. He then began flooding me with so much work, it was impossible for one person to do a good job of it. I stayed back in office till the wee hours to complete work. And I was absolutely sure I would be fired soon for doing such a shoddy job of it.

It was 11:00 pm when my phone rang. I was still in the office. "Hey!" It was Joanna. In response to her chirpy greeting, I said, "I'm at work."

"What??? It's 11 Sanjay, get out of there!"

"My boss is being discriminatory."

"Discriminatory about what? You're a Sanghavi? That is why?"

"My sexuality!"

"Sanjay, I thought you were in an organisation that promoted diversity."

And all Joanna had to say was that magic word for me to finally have a light-bulb moment. The next day I took the head of human resources into confidence and narrated the entire episode. Since I had the opportunity to directly work with the head of human resources briefly before my new boss joined the organisation, she saw me in good light. I was transferred to another team with immediate effect. And my boss vanished three months later. The grapevine was on a high that day. Nobody knew where he went or what happened to him. But I knew. He was fired.

The day Ravi Gill went missing, I crossed paths with the head of my department and smiled at her with gratitude.

CHAPTER 10

Today I am 29 years old.

"Look Rajiv, they really need to know. I'm 29 for crying out loud. All my friends know, my friends' parents know, colleagues at work know, acquaintances know, but they don't know." I was yelling at a high pitched voice.

Rajiv, trying to calm me down said, "Sanjay, why do mom and dad need to know you're gay? It is just going to cause them unnecessary stress."

"But..."

"Listen Sanjay, you've moved out of home, you're leading your independent life without any interference from them, they aren't pressuring you for marriage, so I repeat, why do you need to tell them? And really, god forbid, one of them can't take the news and succumbs to the shock. Then what? How do you think you're going to cope with that? The guilt will override you completely. I'm suggesting what is best for us as a family!"

"So I continue living a lie?"

"It isn't about lying Sanjay; it is about withholding part of the truth; the part that we know can only hurt them."

I have had this discussion with Rajiv numerous times before. I never did agree with his point of view. But in the larger interest of the family and basic respect for my brother I thought that it would be best to refrain from telling my parents the truth about my sexuality.

Honestly, I was tired of the continuous lying or as my brother diplomatically put it, concealing the truth. My sexuality was such an integral part of me and it pained me to know that those very people who raised me, who took care of me, who looked out for me, who played a critical role in my life were completely oblivious to the truth.

When I was 26, mom said, "Sanjay, you are 26, you've never talked about having a girlfriend." I said, "Mom, girlfriends are not talked about." What I really meant to say was, 'I am gay, gay men have boyfriends not girlfriends."

When I was 27, mom said, "Sanjay, so what if you are 27, I don't think you need to move out of home." I said, "Mom, I need my independence. I feel claustrophobic here." What I really meant to say was, 'I am gay, gay men need to learn to live alone.'

When I was 28, mom said, "Sanjay, you are 28, I think you should get married." I said, "Mom, I don't believe in the concept of arranged marriages, if I intend to get married it will be a love marriage." What I really meant to say was, 'I am gay, gay men don't get married.'

That year my parents passed away in an accident. Touching the feet of my parents' lifeless bodies, with tears rolling down my cheeks I finally had the courage to say to them what I had not said for so many years. Sobbing I said, "Mom! dad! I have something to tell you. Please, this does not change me as a person. I'm the same Sanjay you always knew. I am gay!" And on completing that sentence, I fell to the ground and broke down. On seeing me lose control, Rajiv who was holding back his tears the entire time instantly took me into his arms, hugged me and cried.

Rajiv was right; guilt did override me after I came out to my parents. The guilt of not coming out to them while they were still alive haunted me for years.

******

Tilting my head to the right, I was staring at the piece of modern art on the wall trying to make sense of it.

Kavya and I were regulars at Swaroop Café for lunch since it was in close proximity to the office. Swaroop Café was situated in the same premises as Rudraksh Art

Gallery. The ambience of the café was calm, laid back and unconventional. With the menu being reasonably priced, there were exactly 10 tables in the café with each table occupied by people so diverse from each other. You could have a socialite at one table and a labourer at the other; a corporate honcho at one table and a struggling artist at the other. It was pleasantly bizarre how people from such diverse walks of life have all come under one roof. The right side of the café opened up to a beautiful garden with trees, plants, flowers and a little pond. Any kind of greenery in an urban jungle like Mumbai was always a welcome sight. At the café, Kavya had the Special of the Day '*Aloo Paratha*' (Indian delicacy stuffed with potatoes) and I had ordered for my usual favourite Fish N' Chips. After we were done with lunch, while Kavya went to the restroom, I began browsing through the work of art at Rudraksh.

"I love the way this artist has portrayed a balance between hope and pessimism in his work," a voice with a peculiar accent was heard from behind me.

I turned around to lay my eyes on the most handsome man I had seen in my life. The first thing I noticed about him was his light brown eyes and his stubble. He had straight hair, appropriately gelled with a bit of the front nicely falling on his forehead. He seemed exactly two inches taller than me (which would be perfect in a scenario if and when we kissed). The way his chest and biceps were almost ripping through his shirt, it was obvious he worked out a lot. He was very well groomed too. He was wearing a well ironed sparkling blue shirt, a black pin-striped blazer over it, jet black pair of flat-front trousers and finally shiny black leather shoes to complete the ensemble.

Maintaining my composure in front of this highly attractive man, I said, "I'm sorry I'm really not into art. I was just waiting for a friend."

"Thank god! What a relief! I'm not into art either. I just wanted to strike a conversation with you. And thought this would be the best way to start the banter. By the way, I'm Ritwik, Ritwik Kala."

Shaking the hand he had held out, I introduced myself, "Hi Ritwik! I'm Sanjay Sanghavi. It really is a pleasure to meet you."

"This may seem really awkward, but it's how we always did it in the States, do you want to do coffee with me sometime?"

I beamed, handing over my visiting card to him, I said, "I would love to. Call me soon!"

Giving him one last playful smile, I walked towards Kavya who was waiting near the exit. "Who was that piece of eye-candy?" she enquired.

Rolling my eyes I said, "My future husband!" And the both of us giggled.

******

My first date with Ritwik was extremely unusual. "I'll pick you up at 7 am. And make sure you're dressed casual." He called me the day before the weekend. 'Casual?' I thought to myself, 'What did he mean by casual?'

I had no clue what he meant when he said "Dress Casual!" I decided to call Riya for advice. "Hey! It's me!" I said when she answered the phone.

"Hi beautiful! What's up?" she exclaimed.

"Listen! I have a date! And I need advice!"

"You have a date? Who? What? When? I need all the details Mr Sanghavi." After giving her a brief description of Ritwik and how we met, Riya screamed with excitement, "He sounds so nice! I would have dumped Ranveer for him."

We both giggled like little teenage girls. "But I don't know what the fuck he meant by dress casual. I mean who the fuck is casually dressed for the first date. Aren't you supposed to be looking your best on the first date?"

Riya's advice began, "Look, this is what you should do; dress casual but not too casual. Dress nice but not too nice. You know what I mean right?"

You definitely had to know Riya long enough to decode that message. Riya and I had been friends for a while now and so I understood exactly what she meant. "You mean balance it out?" I asked her.

"Precisely! Smart boy you are! Have fun on the date and let me know what happens."

"Pray that this is it for me! I'm tired of these stupid flings. I want to settle down now."

"My fingers are always crossed! And you know the drill right? Expectations should be at level zero and not level twenty!"

"Yes mommy!" And I hung up the phone on Riya.

The next morning, I woke up as early as 5:00 am. After the mandatory morning activities, I looked at my wardrobe. I began rambling to myself, 'Casual, but not too casual! Nice, but not too nice!' I picked up a pair of blue jeans, wore a white tee, put on my sneakers, gelled my hair and suddenly heard a honk. I looked at the clock it was 5 minutes past 7:00 am. I looked outside the balcony window and saw Ritwik gazing in the direction of my apartment sitting in the driver's seat of his black car. I waved out to him and gestured "two minutes' with my fingers.

As soon as I walked towards his car, Ritwik hugged me, gave me a peck on my cheek, "And you're coming trekking like this?" he asked. Ritwik was wearing a tight fitted purple tee, cream-coloured shorts and sneakers with the Adidas logo at the tip of the sole. His muscles were even more prominent today. Trying not to be distracted by his good looks and large muscles, I screamed, "We're going trekking? You didn't tell me that. How am I supposed to assume casual meant clothes for a trek?" Instructing me, he said, "Fine, go and change into clothes meant for a trek now!"

Walking back to my apartment, I grumbled to myself, 'Who treks on the first date? I anyway hate treks. This is so not going to work out. God! When the hell will I find the right guy?'

I put on a pair of shorts, changed into a more casual tee and let the sneakers I was wearing just be. I went back to his car and putting on a phony excited smile I said, "Let's go!"

Ritwik began driving towards our destination which I absolutely had no clue of. "You're not a trekking kind of person, are you?" Ritwik asked me. I genuinely laughed and said, "Not at all!" He smiled and said convincingly, "I'm sure this is a trek you will enjoy." We reached our destination in two hours flat. I really didn't know where the time flew while chatting with Ritwik. In conversation, I found out that he was an orphan who was adopted by an Indian-American couple. He was 31-years-old. He had completed his masters only recently from the Wharton School of Business. He wanted to come back to India because he strongly believed that this is where his roots lie and felt complete here. Professionally, he was currently heading strategy for S&M, one of the leading FMCG (Fast Moving Consumer Goods) companies.

As soon as I got off the car at our destination, I was mesmerised by the natural beauty around me. There was so much peace and serenity, we were surrounded by hills on all sides, all I could see was the colour of trees, plants and flowers and of course the blue sky, the weather was absolutely pleasant and there wasn't a single soul in sight. As soon as I noticed how isolated the place was, out of nowhere, tiny versions of Vikram and Arth popped up on either shoulder of mine.

The scene seemed straight out of a cartoon, Vikram was dressed as the devil and Arth as the angel. 'When will my gay friends let me be?' I thought to myself. Vikram spoke first. Reading my mind he said, "Never! We will hound you till death does us part. Look where you are, not a single soul in sight, must be a bloody gay basher! I hope you are still alive after this trek! I told you there is no such thing as love in the gay community." Arth went next, "Don't listen to this fool! You do what your heart says. If this is destined to turn into love, it will. Go for it!"

"Sanjay, everything fine?" Vikram and Arth vanished into thin air and I was snapped out of the weird comical scene by Ritwik's question.

"Yeah I'm fine. I was lost in the stunning sight around me," I replied back.

Taking my hand into his, Ritwik pointed to the pinnacle of one of the hills and said, "That is where we need to go!"

I looked to the top and sighed, "That is really high up!"

"Don't worry I'm here with you. I'll be by your side till the end."

I smiled and began trekking with Ritwik on my side. The trek was quite a difficult path, it was rocky in most parts and I slipped 'n' times on the way up. Every time I did slip and fall Ritwik held on to me and didn't let go. I wondered why I was cribbing so much about going on this trek, surprisingly, I was enjoying myself thoroughly!

"Here we are!" Ritwik exclaimed on reaching the top. I looked around and was flabbergasted by what I saw. At a distance I saw a river, it was so quiet that we could literally hear the ripples of the calm water flowing. To my right I saw a clump of trees, to my left was another. I saw an eagle swoop down for a drink of water from the river. Little birds continued to chirp as the sun shone on us warmly. I looked toward the blue sky to see the clouds forming different shapes. It took me to my childhood when mom used to ask Rajiv and me to use our imagination and figure out what the cloud was shaping to be. As a kid I saw elephants, cows, fish in the sky. Today I saw signs of freedom, happiness, confidence in the sky.

The sight was absolutely striking. I exclaimed, "Ritwik, this is so beautiful. I love it!" Ritwik came close to me, slowly took my face into his palms and kissed me. It didn't matter how sweaty and damp our bodies were from the trek. We smiled when we kissed. It was obvious we were happy in the moment. We continued kissing and smiling till the sun set.

On our way home, I gazed at the man on the driver's seat. I looked at Ritwik and hoped that this would turn out the way I wanted it to. As soon as I reached home, my first date with Ritwik came to an end with a peck on the lips. While I waved good bye as he drove away, I sighed and said to myself, 'God! Let this be the right guy!'

******

It had been two months since my first date with Ritwik. He and I had begun spending all our free time together. Since we worked in the same vicinity, we met for lunch every day; we went for tennis lessons three working days of the week, went to the gym for the remaining two working days and casually spent the weekends at each others' apartments or trekking in the hills.

It is very rare for my friends to get along with any of the men I had dated in the past. I always held my friends' opinions in high regard. And that is the reason my friends were key drivers in breaking up past relationships I had. But Ritwik was loved by everybody. Right from my friends from Graduation College to Dilu and Kelly to Arth and Vikram to my friends from TISS, everybody loved Ritwik. "What a catch!" Rakhi had said. "He is such a sweet guy!" Sonali had said. "Yummy!" Kelly had said. I was elated by my friends' reactions about Ritwik because I really liked him myself. Correction! Actually I think I was falling in love with Ritwik.

I never introduced any of my boyfriends to Rajiv and Mahi unless I was 100% sure that the boy I was dating had the potential to be 'My Partner'. So, they had never met any of my boyfriends in the past. At that time of the year, Rajiv and Mahi were in the city visiting and I thought this would be a good opportunity to put Ritwik through the final and most important test of acceptance.

While I was buttoning Ritwik's shirt, I began rambling, "Mahi is easy. Rajiv is tough. Rajiv can be inappropriately funny at times. Just laugh off his condescending jokes. Remember everybody does not have a good sense of humour. My brother is worried about me so don't be surprised if he asks you stupid questions around what you do and how much money you earn."

"Sanjay, baby, I'll handle this. I know how important this is to you. What is important to you is important to me too. Don't worry I will charm your family." Ritwik winked at me which surprisingly calmed me down. I believed Ritwik. I did breathe a sigh of relief and headed towards the most anxious dinner I have had in years with the man I loved in tow. It had been two months since we were dating but Ritwik and I had never said the three words to each other - 'I love you.' I guess the both of us were waiting for the other to say it. At the end of the day, we were two men dating, egos were bound to clash. I know for a fact that I was an egoistic bastard, and was waiting for him to say that he loved me before I said it to him.

At Rajiv and Mahi's, Ritwik worked his charm like he had never worked it before. He said all the right things, complimented Mahi's food and looks, he also appreciated the fact that she was in such a noble profession addressing her as Dr Mahi playfully. The entire night, he talked sports and stocks with Rajiv and he also laughed at all of Rajiv's annoying jokes. Mahi gave me a thumbs up from the kitchen door whereas Rajiv messaged me that night, saying, 'Great guy! Hold on to him!'

I was ecstatic on the way home. I was also on a high because of all the drinks I had consumed on account of my anxiety. I began rambling again, kissing Ritwik all over his face while he was driving, I exclaimed, "Ritwik you were awesome tonight! I am so happy! Rajiv and Mahi loved you. What a relief! Rajiv and Mahi mean everything to me. I mean if they didn't like you I would have been so disillusioned, I wouldn't have known what to do." Ritwik knew how important this night was to me and smiled while I continued chattering.

"You fine with a drive? Or you want to go home?" Ritwik asked me.

"Yes drive! Let's go for a drive!" I responded.

Ritwik drove to an empty space. The spot was absolutely deserted. There was nothing around. All that was there was the ground below, the stars shining in the dark sky above and the two of us. If I wasn't that drunk, I would have been in complete admiration of the romantic secluded spot. However, in my drunkenness I yelled, "How do you know all these eerie quiet places? I'm sure you must have brought all the boys you wanted to have sex with here." I began laughing hysterically. "Oh! I'm so funny!" I proclaimed.

Ritwik silenced me. Taking from his cue, I put my finger on my lips to shut myself up. "Sanjay, I've wanted to tell you something. You're one of the nicest, funniest, good looking men I've met. I feel complete with you. I feel happy when I'm with you. I don't feel the need for anything else when I'm with you. I just needed you to know that I love you." And with those three words, I felt a tear in my eye. "Well, I'm a little drunk for this. But who cares, you love me!" "Do you have something to say back to me?" Ritwik nervously asked me. "Do I?" I asked Ritwik back. How I wish I wasn't this drunk that night. Thankfully I realised what an ass I was being and finally said, "Oh! Yes of course! I love you too, Ritwik! I loved you from the day I met you at the art gallery. You are such a wonderful person and you are an even more wonderful human being. I love you so much!" And then I began bawling like a baby. "Don't worry! These are happy tears!" I continued rambling. "Shut me up! Shut me up now!" I yelled.

And with that instruction, Ritwik kissed me. We did have sex numerous times before that, but that day we didn't just have sex, we made love. We made love in the open, under the stars. I slowly unbuttoned his shirt while he kissed me. He held me tight while I felt his strong arms. He turned me around and kissed my naked back. He slowly caressed my butt and thighs. I turned around again and kissed his chest and stomach. I bit his ear and neck. After an extensive indulgence in foreplay, he slowly took me in and we let ourselves go.

That night, we didn't go home. We spent the night with our naked bodies closely held tight looking into each others' eyes and smiling.

CHAPTER 11

Today I am 33 years old.

"No you're not going and that is my final decision." Ritwik was yelling at the top of his voice.

"Your final decision? When did you become the final decision maker in this house?" I yelled back.

It had been four years since Ritwik and I had been romantically involved and it had been a year since we had moved in together. I remember Ritwik had spent weeks trying to figure out how to ask me to move in with him. He wanted to make it special; he tried surprising me by placing the key to his apartment in my glass of wine. I was livid on finding a key in my glass at one of the city's finest restaurants. Before Ritwik could explain, I was yelling at the restaurant's manager, "You place a piece of metal in my glass? What were you trying to do, kill me? What if I had swallowed the key? This is absolutely appalling! I never expected this from a first grade restaurant like yours." Ritwik was so embarrassed; he spent the entire night apologising to the management.

I was having a conversation with the head of Human Resources and my current boss, Karnika Patel, in her cabin. "Sanjay, we are very happy with the kind of traction you have been able to build with the business teams here. The way you handled the restructuring of the agency business was absolutely impeccable. I mean who would have thought of such fantastic alignment of people to the new model in only a span of a week other than you." I held my head high with pride while my boss complimented me. Karnika continued, "It is important that we focus on the development of key talent like you. That's why I would like to discuss a career opportunity with you." In my career with WSU Life spanning seven years, I had already had the opportunity to see five different roles. I had handled business support, performance management, training and organisational development. I really didn't know what to expect next. I always thought my next career move would be Karnika's role as head Human Resources. Now, clearly that's not happening. "We know you're ready to head the function, but before you head Human Resources for such a large business in India, we thought it would be a good idea to allow you to test the waters first." I was getting a little impatient with the build up to the finale. I thought it would be a good idea to intervene so that it would hurry my boss up to come to the point, "I'm sorry Karnika, I don't understand." Karnika then finally said, "The business in the Philippines is not as large as it is in India. Sanjay, the management and I would like you to head Human Resources for WSU Life there. The bancassurance model is struggling there and I think your people input will be key to the model's success there." I was taken aback; I didn't expect this and didn't know what to say. "Philippines?" I asked. "Look Sanjay, it isn't a permanent arrangement. This will be a short term assignment for two years. And the plan is for you to come back and head the function here in India." My career has always been extremely important to me and I was obviously thrilled with the opportunity. "Karnika, I am truly honoured for you to think of me as worthy of the opportunity but moving countries is a big decision and I would need some time to come back to you." Karnika then said, "Come on Sanjay, what is there to think? Opportunities like this aren't given to everybody. And it isn't like you have family here." "But I will need to discuss this with Ritwik." I said in response. "Fine, let me know by Friday. I need to let the management know by this weekend. And really Sanjay, you are two men living together at the end of the day, what is more important to the two of you than your careers? Ritwik will understand."

But, Ritwik didn't understand. All Ritwik understood

was that we were a couple and a couple is supposed to stay together and not apart. While we argued that morning, Ritwik and I continued yelling not coming to a mutual conclusion. "Go to hell Sanjay! Fuck it! Do whatever you want!" Ritwik roared before slamming the door and storming out of the house.

Ritwik only came back home post midnight. As soon as he entered, I screamed, "Ritwik! Where the fuck have you been? I have been worried sick! Why the hell do you only think about yourself all the time?" Ritwik without saying a word, walked towards the couch, switched on the television and sat down. "Ritwik! I am talking to you!" I continued screaming. My words full of anger continued to fall on deaf ears, however I didn't stop yelling. "So that is your plan? You're just going to continue ignoring me! We aren't going to talk?" When I was finally sure that I wouldn't get any kind of response from him, I decided to surrender. Not even looking in his direction, I walked to our bedroom and went to sleep.

The following morning, I was awakened with a peck on the forehead. Stretching my hands out, and opening my eyes I saw Ritwik smiling with a cup of coffee in his hand. His smile was infectious, but I knew I was upset with him so I decided to just snatch the cup of coffee from his hand and murmured, "Thanks!"

"Sanjay, I've been thinking!" Ritwik initiated conversation.

'It was about time' I thought to myself. "And...." I said aloud.

"This is a good move for your career. I think you should take up the opportunity in Philippines. It is only a matter of two years. We'll survive this."

"You really think so?" I questioned doubtfully. And that made me realise that I was still unsure if this was the right path to take.

"Yup! Plus we'll get tips from Kritika and Rahul on how to survive a long distance relationship." He smiled, reassuring me that we really would survive this.

A few weeks later, I was at the airport, bidding goodbye to all my friends. "Don't forget us you bastard!" Saif screamed while I hugged Rakhi. I was too emotional to say anything at the time, pounding my fist against my chest and pointing my finger to my group of friends I indicated that I loved them. Rajiv like any older brother gave me tons of advice while bidding me adieu. "Be careful of the pimps on the street. They're all over the place in the Philippines. And if you're ever short of cash let me know. And uncle Mehta is in Manila too. Reach out to him in case of any help required." Like always, I smiled patiently through my brother's advice. I hugged Mahi and kissed my two-year-old nephew Rehaan. I looked at Rehaan and pointing a finger at him I instructed, "Listen champ! Take good care of mom and dad in my absence! And if they trouble you too much, you know Manila isn't too far away." Rehaan beamed through my funny expressions not understanding a word I was saying.

Last in the queue to say his goodbye was Ritwik. "You save the toughest goodbye for the end, huh?" I questioned Ritwik trying to put on a brave face. Ritwik just stared at me. He looked like a ten-year-old child with a frown that was almost shifting to turn into a full-fledged bawl. "So are you going to say anything? Or do I just go?" I asked trying to make the farewell a little easier for both of us. Ritwik hugged me tightly and began to cry. "I love you Sanjay! I'm going to miss you so much!" With tears rolling down my face as well, I said, "Me too Ritwik! We'll survive this! You remember you said that!" The parting began to take a toll on me. I couldn't take it any longer. Slowly pushing Ritwik away, I headed in the direction of the Emigration counter.

While I turned to see my family and friends one last time before I left, I saw Joanna hugging Ritwik tightly consoling him. 'We'll be fine!' I said smiling to myself and headed to board Flight AI 354 to Manila, Philippines.

******

While I sipped my coffee at the local deli, I was distracted by the front page newspaper article a man was holding up and reading on the next table. It read: 'Terror Attack in Mumbai, India - 180 feared dead.' Reading the headlines, I immediately called Ritwik. "Hi baby! Everything is fine right?" I enquired on hearing his voice at the other end of the line. "Yeah it is! Don't worry. All of us are fine here. Now listen sweetheart I'm at work. I'll call you later." And with that, Ritwik hastily hung up the phone. I went back to sipping my coffee when the man behind the newspaper peered and asked me, "You from Mumbai?" I nodded in the affirmative. I wasn't in the mood for small talk and so looked away from the man.

Suddenly, he walked over the table I was at and asked, "May I?" Giving one of my non-genuine smiles, I pointed at the vacant chair and said, "Please, go ahead!" By the end of the forced conversation, I thought of Victor as a nice guy. 'There was no harm in being friends with this guy.' I thought to myself. It had been three months since I had moved to Manila and I was kind of lonely, I had no friends, no social circle. Victor was a 28-year-old good-looking man born and brought up in the Philippines. He wrote for a living and was a regular at the deli since he believed that his inspiration for his writing came from regular people sipping coffee at this very place. "For instance, you just played a part in creating a subject around my next piece of work." He told me. "A foreigner in an unfamiliar country just receives the news of a loved one back home passing away in a terrorist attack. What do you think?" "Interesting!" I said in response to his concept.

That night Victor and I went to watch a movie. "Hysterical! I loved the humour in Juno. I could watch it again and again." I told Victor while we were walking back home. "Well this is me!" I said on reaching my destination pointing to the apartment building on the right. "This was so much fun! We should go bowling next weekend!" I said excitedly to my new found friend. Completely out of the blue, Victor groped me and tried to kiss me. As an immediate reflex, I pushed him away and yelled, "Victor! What the hell do you think you are doing?"

He was obviously embarrassed by what he had just done. But while I continued to look at a regretful Victor, a bizarre feeling overcame me. Victor suddenly looked attractive, in fact he looked striking. I could visualise him with no clothes on and us making out in my apartment. It had been three months since I had been away from Ritwik and for Heaven's sake I was a man at the end of the day. 21 more months without sex suddenly seemed like an extremely tough challenge to me.

But in that split second, thankfully love won over lust. I asked Victor to leave and never see me again. I didn't feel the need to tell Ritwik about the incident. He was already insecure; he had never been to the Philippines in his life and always pictured me in this exotic locale with a bunch of Asian boys feeding me grapes. And at the end of the day, nothing really happened except for the realisation that 21 months ahead is going to be tough.

******

"It is getting really tough. I really need your advice! How do we survive this? All our conversations end up in fights. I love Ritwik so much but this is really stressing me out." I was talking to Kritika on the phone seeking her advice.

"Sanjay, long distance relationships are obviously tough. It really seems like both of you aren't putting in the effort. Trust me, and I speak from personal experience, this won't even last one more day if only one of you is willing to work at it. Like I always say, you guys need to make this last together. It is a joint effort!"

What followed were a bunch of practical tips from Kritika that I immediately carried out like a diligent student as soon as I hung up the phone on her.

That night, tip number one was put into action.

"Don't try to move, this ship has been hijacked! I am Pirate Jones!" I said while speaking to Ritwik over the phone.

"Sanjay, why are you acting so juvenile? What nonsense are you up to?" Ritwik asked me while he laughed.

"Don't laugh mister! You do not want to mess with Pirate Jones!"

"So what does Pirate Jones want from me?" Ritwik asked playing along.

"Pirate Jones wants you to take your shirt off and be ashamed of what a bad boy you have been lately." I said in an extremely mischievous tone.

That conversation ended with the best phone sex I had ever had in my entire lifetime. Thanks to Kritika's practical tips my dwindling relationship with Ritwik did survive.

We wrote to each other every night detailing out every activity in the course of the day right from the work out in the gym to the number of times we visited the restroom. Saturday nights were fixed as 'movie date night' where we simultaneously watched the same DVD together while we chatted. Sunday dinners were exotic, we dressed up and ordered in different cuisines - one Sunday it would be Sushi the next it would be Mexican. And of course, we did extremely wacky stuff for each other on special occasions. On his 35th birthday, Ritwik sent me 31 pairs of underwear and a message that read, 'This is for all the years we missed out on for you not coming into my life earlier.' And lastly, the six monthly visits were a godsend to the both of us.

One night while I was checking my email, I smiled on noticing an email from Kritika. The subject line of the email read, 'Gift from Ritwik!' I quickly downloaded the mail and saw a picture of Kritika holding up a frame. I zoomed into the frame she was holding; it was a certificate placed in a beautifully carved wooden casing. The certificate read, 'A Big Hug Awarded to Kritika - Future Author of the Best-Seller - How to Successfully Survive a Long Distance Relationship! With Lots of Love from, Sanjay and Ritwik!'

I looked up towards the sky and happily yelled, "Thank you god!"

CHAPTER 12

Today I am 35 years old.

Ritwik and I were awakened by continuous pounding on the door. "What time is it?" Ritwik asked me with one eye open. I picked up my mobile phone to see what time it was. "It is 2:00 am. Who the hell is it at this time of the night?" I responded in a groggy tone.

I opened the door to see a shaken Arth and his boyfriend Vishal. Arth met Vishal online three years ago. It was truly love at first sight; they proclaimed their love for each other right after their first date and had been going steady ever since. "Get ready now! We need to head to Vikram's!" Arth was screaming at the top of his voice. "But what is wrong? Vikram is fine right?" I asked sounding nervous. "Vikram called sounding absolutely miserable. He was crying. I kept probing, he wasn't saying anything. He just asked you and me to come to his house now." Ritwik stepped out of the bedroom rubbing his right eye, "What is wrong? Everything alright?" I quickly pulled him into the room screaming with a sense of urgency in my voice, "We need to head to Vikram's NOW!"

On reaching Vikram's house, we found the door to his apartment open. It was pitch black inside. "Vikram!" Arth and I called out while Ritwik opened the door. There was no response. Vishal switched on the light in the hall way and hollered, "Vikram, it's us, are you there?" Arth and I cautiously walked into Vikram's bedroom and switched on the light. In the corner of the bedroom, Vikram was sitting crawled up against the wall on the floor stark naked with a piece of paper in his hand. Ritwik instantly picked up the blanket from the bed and wrapped it around him. Arth and I were scared out of our wits. We didn't know how to react at the sight. Vikram looked up in our direction and began wailing loudly. While Ritwik and Vishal stepped out of the room giving the three of us our privacy, Arth walked towards Vikram, bent down, slowly patted his back and asked, "What is wrong Vikram? What happened? You can tell us! It is only Sanjay and me." Vikram squirmed when Arth touched him; he then handed over to me the piece of paper he was holding.

That piece of paper was a blood report from the neighbouring Asha Clinic. Right in the middle of the page in bold letters it read, 'TESTED: HIV Positive'. My spontaneous reaction was, "It is an error! How can you be so sure? I am certain the clinic has made a mistake." Vikram shouting and sobbing at the same time shrieked, "No it isn't! It is the third blood test I've taken!" Arth hugged Vikram in the spur of the moment. Vikram pushed Arth back and continued yelling, "Move away! Don't touch me! You'll get the bug from me!" Arth and I were saddened looking at Vikram in a state like this. Vikram was the carefree, happy-go-lucky one from the group. It was heart-wrenching to see him like this. We couldn't control our tears. I screamed while crying, "Nothing is going to happen to you! There is medication to control this. We're going to the doctor tomorrow. We're not going to let you die so easily." Vikram from being hopping mad turned to being hysterically distressed. Folding his hands together, he looked towards the two of us and pleaded while sobbing, "Please help me guys! I do not want to die. I'm only 36. My niece loves me so much. Who is going to teach her to play the piano?" Arth responded, "We're here Vikram! We're not going to let anything happen to you. We promise we are going to help you live"

I couldn't take it anymore; I stepped outside the room and began bawling. Ritwik hugged me and tried consoling me, "Babe, it is going to be alright! Don't worry! We're going to take Vikram to the best doctor around. He will live." That was the first time in my six years with Ritwik I didn't believe what he had just said.

******

The following day I fixed an appointment for Vikram with one of the renowned doctors in the city employed at one of the largest hospitals - Dr Anwarali Shaikh.

At 4:00 pm that evening, Arth, Vikram and I occupied three chairs at the fag end of the waiting room. I tried to remain optimistic while we waited for Vikram's turn to come but the sight around us was not helping at all. In front of us, sat a little anxious girl whose foot was the size of a large boulder, to our right was a young man who coughed up blood into his handkerchief and to our left was a mentally challenged woman on a wheel chair, her head was tilted to the right at all times while she continuously stared at nothing. Even though the waiting room was not buoyant at all, I wanted to be hopeful for Vikram. Looking in his direction, I smiled holding his hand. He smiled back. Suddenly, our attention was diverted to the voice at the reception table. "Mr Vikram! Dr Shaikh will see you now!" The nurse hollered.

Dr Shaikh's office was as big as the dining room in our apartment. He had a large-sized table adorned with pretty pots of plants. Vikram sat in the chair meant for the patient right across Dr Shaikh. Arth and I occupied the couch towards the left of the room against the wall placed parallel to the king-sized table. Dr Shaikh pointing his Mont Blanc pen to Vikram's blood report asked, "So, Vikram, how many times have you tested for this?"

Vikram looked the doctor in the eye and said, "Thrice!"

"I need you to be completely honest for me to help you." Dr Shaikh warned Vikram before he began his interrogation.

"I understand!"

"Are you into drugs? Any needles you've been using?"

"No!"

"Have you gone through any blood transfusion in the recent past?"

"No!"

"Any unsafe sex?"

"Only safe sex."

"Well a condom is not 100% safe, Mr Vikram! I hope you are aware."

"Yes I am."

"Have you had multiple partners?"

Vikram looked towards us seeking our consent, Arth and I nodded giving Vikram a go ahead to tell the doctor the truth. Vikram looking the doctor in the eye again said "Yes! I have had sex with multiple partners."

"Have these been homosexual encounters?"

Arth and I were clearly stunned by the question. This time without looking at us, Vikram responded, "Yes."

Dr Shaikh leaned back on his chair, now holding the Mont Blanc pen between his teeth said, "Mr Vikram unfortunately under **Section 377*** of the Indian Penal code I will have to deny you any kind of medical support."

I intervened, "What are you talking about doctor? Section 377 talks about intercourse against the order of nature. It doesn't talk about denying medical treatment."

Dr Shaikh cut my rambling short, "My friend, I can be jailed for treating Vikram since he has caught the virus through unnatural sex. In fact it would be a criminal offence if I do not report a patient with an anal sexually transmitted infection. However, I am under the oath of doctor-patient confidentiality so I will not report this. You may all now leave my office."

"People like you should be arrested for murder," Arth screamed on our way out.

"And people like you should be killed in public," Dr Shaikh yelled back.

On our way home, Arth and I were consoling a stressed Vikram. "Listen Vikram, we'll find another doctor. This guy was a jerk. Really, don't worry." I said while driving the car. Honestly, though, I was worried;

my impending optimism was killed by the incident today. 'What if nobody is willing to treat Vikram?' I kept asking myself.

******

"Sanjay! Come here quickly!" Ritwik yelled while I was getting ready for work in the bedroom. I rushed to the room Ritwik was in and asked, "What? What happened?" Ritwik handed me the newspaper pointing to the front page:

Homosexual denied medical treatment on account of Section 377

Monday, June 20, Mumbai: Thirty-six-year old Vikram Goel, a resident of Mumbai was denied medical treatment by a well renowned physician, Dr. Anwarali Shaikh at one of the city's leading hospitals for having contracted HIV through a homosexual encounter. Our source on the condition of anonymity said, "Once Dr. Shaikh confirmed that the patient had contracted the virus through a homosexual act, he denied the patient medical treatment on account of section 377." Mr. Bal Subramanian, the public relations officer for the hospital also recorded his statement for the press, "We are currently investigating the case. It is too early to make a comment on the way forward." Both Mr. Goel and Dr. Shaikh remained unavailable for comment.

On reading the news snippet, I exclaimed, "Oh God!"

Ritwik and I rushed to Vikram's house to find a hoard of reporters almost breaking down the door to his apartment. We managed our way through the pack and rang the door bell to the apartment. Arth peeped through the key hole and let us in. We literally pushed back the reporters who were trying to barge into the apartment. As soon as we entered, Vikram with his hands on his head kept screaming hysterically, "I am doomed! I am doomed!"

"What happened? I can't understand." I yelled sounding all confused.

"Yeah! I thought that doctor said he would keep it confidential." Ritwik questioned sounding as confused as I did.

Arth looked in Vishal's direction and said, "Vishal, will you clear it out for them?"

Vishal worked with a media firm and always had the inside news on any scoop. "I got to know this morning, it seems a nurse overheard the conversation you had and let it out to the press for big money."

"What a bitch!" I exclaimed spontaneously.

All of us decided to stay back at Vikram's to provide some kind of solace to him in the middle of that madness. Vikram had not gotten any sleep for days, while he was finally able to catch up on some sleep in his bedroom; I shut the door and joined the rest of the gang who were chatting up in the living room.

"Can you believe what people can do for money?" Arth was in the midst of conversation.

"I swear, it is really pathetic," I interrupted supporting Arth's comment.

It had been a couple of hours since we had begun talking. I decided to check on Vikram in the bedroom. As I opened the bedroom door, I saw him crouched up on his bed, staring at a blade in his hand. As soon as he heard the click of the door open, he turned around. He half smiled at me. Showing me the blade, Vikram voiced his sentiment angrily, "It's pathetic! Why do I even have to think of doing this to myself? I can't believe it! I actually thought of killing myself. Because of what? Because I'm considered a freak in this stupid country! Because some age old law thinks that homosexuality is against the order of nature! Because I'm going against tradition!" Vikram's tone got louder and angrier by the second. "Tradition? What fuck'n tradition? I had the fuck'n guts to choose to be who I am. I was being true to myself. I'm not accountable to these hypocritical assholes who are just bullies in the disguise of propagators of Indian tradition. Also, some bloody jackass didn't have the balls to tell me that he was infected and I have to kill myself. For what? Why should I?" I slowly took the blade away from

Vikram's hand and gently stroked the back of his head to calm him down. "It's alright Vikram! We've all made choices. The last thing you want to do is regret the choice you've made. You chose to be true to yourself. And I'm so glad you didn't choose the easy way out of running away from all this by killing yourself." I wiped the tears from Vikram's face, "Come on, I think you need something to eat. We're all starving as well. And you know how cranky that Arth gets without food." Vikram caught hold of my hand, just as I was about to head to open the door to his room. "Thanks Sanjay! You do know you're an absolute sweetheart. And you know what, I thank god I'm gay. Do you want to know the real reason behind why I refrained from killing myself?" I looked bewildered. "What? What is that?" "I love my green painted walls way too much; I couldn't bear to see any blood stains on them even before I died." I smiled.

******

As the days went by, the media went even more berserk. Non-availability of statements from both Vikram and Dr Shaikh led to more curiosity being generated around the case. And of course, the grapevine was at its wildest best.

My friend Vikram Goel was the current hot topic in the city which didn't just seem to die down. Be it the news anchor facilitating debates on television, "Today's topic for discussion around the Vikram Goel case, 'Are we killing homosexuals in the name of age old laws and tradition?' Be it in crowded trains, "*Arre*, have you heard the latest? It seems that Goel fellow was having an affair with the doctor. The doctor's wife found out and so cooked up this story and took it to the media." Be it on the radio, "Good morning Mumbai! This is RJ Shania and we're asking you to participate in the 'Save Vikram Goel' drive at Gurgaon Chowpatty this Sunday!" Be it at movements driven by LGBT organisations, "Down with Section 377! We are also human! Down with Dr Shaikh!

Save Vikram Goel!" Be it at government offices, "These gay men have really stooped to new levels. See how they're using diseases to garner sympathy!"

I knew Vikram too well and wasn't surprised when he went missing after a few days. I don't know how he managed to get out of the country without any hullabaloo created by the media. I guess we gay men are quite well-networked after all. He did however leave a note addressed to Arth and myself.

Sanjay and Arth,

Don't get pissed off! I'm sure you guys already knew I would do this but I'm telling you anyway. I've left the country and heading to London to regain my lost sanity.

I'm sorry for not speaking to you before I left. These guys from the media are like peering hawks, just waiting for me to make a move. There was no way in hell I could contact you, so I left you a note. Ain't I the sweetest? ;)

I want to thank you for always being there when you were needed and even when you were not needed. Remember the time that I tried to get rid of you guys because I had a hot date waiting? That was hilarious! I could have killed the both of you at the time!

I had always been a non-believer in love, but looking at the two of you now, you have changed my mind. I could never have let you know that while I was there, I have my principles, you see. But what the hell! Ritwik and Vishal are awesome guys, hold on to them for as long as you can.

I also realised that I have always been in love. I'm in love with the two of you! Now stop crying, I am beginning to tear up just looking at you.

I don't know how many days I have left to live, but I'm going to make sure I have a blast before I die. I am sorry for just running away like this. I guess I was not strong enough. And please don't ever blame yourselves for my leaving. This was not an impulsive decision, it was well thought out. I made the choice as soon as I knew I had become headline news.

Me being me, you don't have to miss me too much because I will always be there in spirit even after I die. Keep the love alive!

Always remember me,

Vikram

Arth and I had tears in our eyes by the time I finished reading the letter aloud. I guess I would have done the same thing if I was in Vikram's place.

A day before my 36th birthday, I received the news of Vikram passing away. On hearing the news, I strangely felt guilty for a very long time, 'Did we really keep our promise? Did we do enough to help Vikram live?'

CHAPTER 13

Today I am 39 years old.

The décor was plain gorgeous. As soon as you entered the large space, you would be awestruck by the rich colours, the gracefully dressed guests and of course the aroma of fancy cuisines. The mix of roses, carnations and daisies delicately placed in traditional vases on each table gave the venue an elegant feel. The tables were covered with manually designed rich red tablecloth. Large white marble standees placed strategically across the site made you feel like you were in a palace. The walls were nicely draped with colourful *dupattas* - red, orange, yellow. The servers wearing shiny white coats and black trousers were doling out exotic cocktails. The buffet spread was massive. To my right lay Chinese, authentic *Mughlai* and Italian pastas. To my left were a series of appetisers, five different kinds of soups and a dessert spread as wide as river Nile. Right in the middle of this spectacular setting was a red carpet sprinkled with yellow rose petals that led you to the stage where you could pass on good wishes to the couple.

Saif was the last among my friends to get married. His girlfriend of many years always got cold feet whenever he asked her to marry him. She finally agreed to get married, however, not to him, but to his cousin Omar. Only a year ago, Saif met Aarti, a 35-year-old divorcee while he was away on a business trip in Morocco. Two weeks ago, he asked her to marry him and she responded with a 'yes' without even blinking an eye. "I thought she'd agree after a couple of years. Nobody agrees to get married to me that quickly, I'm spooked out!" He exclaimed anxiously while sharing the news with us.

While I sat at the table occupied by all my happily married friends with lovely kids - Joanna, Rakhi and Javed - I looked at the couple on stage in wonder. A series of thoughts started running through my mind, 'Will gay marriages in India ever be legal? All my friends are married, including Ditzy Dilu. Will I ever get married? Will I have a beautiful wedding like this? Will I have kids?' Ritwik tapped me on the shoulder and transported me out of musings and into the real world. With the nod of his head he was checking if everything was alright with me. I half smiled in response to his nod and held his hand. I continued looking at the venue, the food, the décor, the couple on stage with a mixed bag of envy and happiness. The flurry of emotions just left me depressed at the end of it. 'I am supposed to be happy for my friends and not go green with jealousy? I am being a bad friend.' This thought left me feeling ashamed of myself.

On our way home, Ritwik and I didn't speak. We had been together long enough for him to understand when I just wanted to be by myself.

About a week later, on a sluggish Saturday, I spent the entire day lazing around, reading books and watching television. Ritwik on the other hand, was away at work. As soon as the clock struck five, I started getting ready. That evening, we had to set out to his cousin Rajat's house warming and I had to pick Ritwik up from his office at 6:30 pm.

Our chauffer Ram drove for a leading film actor before he began driving for us. He was a young 25-year-old who had moved to the big bad city of Mumbai when he was 21 from a small village in the south. He always shared interesting gossip from his last job and that always kept Ritwik and I entertained when we didn't have each other for company in the car. Today I laughed while he told me of the time his previous boss' wife caught her husband having a threesome with his male make-up artist and another leading actress.

Soon, we were stationed outside a big palatial entrance with a large board on top of the doorway that read S&M in bold letters. While Ritwik walked towards the car, I felt a sense of pride when I saw employees, colleagues, security guards, gardeners, everybody showering respect on the man I loved, the deputy CEO at S&M.

While he got into the car, he gently kissed me on the cheek and asked Ram how he was doing. "*Badhiya Sahab*! Mein abhi Sanjay Sahab ko ek interesting kissa suna raha tha." (Great sir! I just narrated an interesting anecdote to Sanjay Sir) He responded with glee while Ritwik smiled. "Someone smells nice today," said Ritwik snuggling up to me.

"So where is Rajat's new house?" I asked him while Ram drove through roads that seemed unfamiliar to me.

"We'll be there soon! He knows you have great taste, so he doesn't want me to discuss his house with you at all - either location or interiors. He wants you to give him an unbiased opinion." Ritwik responded.

"And what if I hate it?"

Ritwik gave one of his impish smiles and said, "Sanjay, I know you can lie when you have to. So you'll manage to keep Rajat happy."

Finally, close to 8 pm, Ram turned into a parking lot. One of the attendants at the parking lot opened the door for me and greeted me enthusiastically, "Welcome Mr Sanghavi! It is an absolute pleasure for us to have you here."

I looked towards Ritwik with complete bewilderment. Ritwik smiled, took my hand in his and walked me to an open area. It was a stunning beach complete with white sand, beautifully carved boulders and pretty shells visibly spread over the surface.

In one corner next to a food and wine counter was Sunaina (our maid) dressed in a new sparkling *Kanjeevaram* sari and on the other corner was a young, muscular man wearing just a cowboy hat and a pair of shorts, holding a guitar. As soon as he saw us, he began playing the guitar singing 'Everything I do' by Bryan Adams. In each corner of that secluded space a large lamp was placed allowing the light to fall on the round wooden table placed right in the centre of the beach. Two hand-crafted chairs were placed next to the table with a candle lit right in the middle along with purple carnations (which happened to be my favourite flowers).

In complete confusion, I looked towards Ritwik and screamed, "Where is Rajat's house? And what is Sunaina doing here?"

"Babe, just walk with me," he responded calmly.

We walked towards the round wooden table. As soon as we reached the table, the guitarist stopped playing and walked away. It really seemed like this entire event was planned to the tee and it began to frustrate me that I didn't know what the hell was going on.

Ritwik looked into my eyes with that dreamy stare that I was attracted to the first time we met. Holding both my hands he said, "Sanjay, it has been ten years since we met. Every single moment I have spent with you has been absolutely memorable. I was so happy when you hugged me through the good times and happier when you hugged me even tighter during the bad. You are my support system, you are my love, you make me feel complete. I can't imagine spending a day without you." I tried holding back tears as Ritwik spoke. He then bent on one knee and asked me, "Will you marry me?"

I am known for being a killjoy and I lived up to it. "But how? Gay marriages aren't legal here?"

"Sanjay, sweetheart just answer the question, I have everything planned."

Unable to hold back tears anymore, I cried and screamed "Yes I will Mr Kala!"

And then we kissed. The guitarist came back in our proximity playing 'You look wonderful tonight' by Eric Clapton. We danced slowly holding each other tightly. After that, Sunaina served us the most wonderful food she had ever cooked. She knew this was a special moment for both of us.

While we kissed, danced, ate, drank, we just didn't want the night to end.

******

"Nepal! That is the place we're going to exchange our vows!" Ritwik initiated conversation the next morning while we were still cuddling after a good night sleep.

"Huh?" I responded sounding all dazed.

"I told you I had everything planned, right. Look Sanjay, we obviously cannot be legally married here. But I think it is important that we at least have a ceremony that celebrates our love. In Nepal, gay marriages are legal, so we'll exchange our vows there. We then come back to India even though not legally married here but at least with the feeling closest to it. I know it may not be the real thing but..."

I cut Ritwik short, "I love the idea. Sounds perfect!"

The next few weeks went in planning our wedding - the dates, the invitation cards, the list of invitees, the venue, the food, the décor, everything.

Exactly six weeks later, we were on a flight to Katmandu to celebrate our love.

Traditionally, neither Ritwik nor I had to be given away so we decided to walk together to the podium where we were to exchange our vows. The venue seemed straight out from a fairy tale. Our wedding was carried out in the middle of the forest in Chitwan. Close to 40 guests rode on elephants while being brought to the quadrangle for the ceremony from the cottages they were put up in. The guests were seated in chairs that were made from bamboo. The quadrangle was surrounded by trees, plants and bushes on all sides. We could hear the constant chirping of birds. To our right at a distance was an exotic waterfall that flowed into an adjacent river. Herds of deer were frequently seen sipping water from the river. The four corners of the quadrangle were splurged with white carnations placed on standees made of sandstone. While Ritwik and I walked towards the stage, I whispered into his ears, "Thank god for Stephen!" Stephen, Joanna's husband was an event manager and helped us with the décor. The stage was stunning; with a white backdrop the floor was covered with red, yellow and orange rose petals. I looked around to notice all my friends. Joanna blew me a flying kiss; Dilu waved hysterically at me; Riya beamed with tears in her eyes. I smiled at all my friends and held Ritwik's hand tightly while we stepped on to the stage. The day was extremely special to us and so Ritwik and I thought it would be apt for someone like Rajiv to conduct the ceremony; Rajiv smiled at both of us before he began the ceremony. "We are gathered here today to celebrate the love of Ritwik Kala and Sanjay Sanghavi." While Rajiv continued with the proceedings Ritwik and I continued staring dreamily at each other. "The grooms may now kiss." Rajiv finally said. Without wasting a second, Ritwik and I kissed. That moment was magical.

Back at our cottage suite, Ritwik and I snuggled while we slept. All of this seemed like a pleasant dream, I was only praying that I never woke up. Ritwik reading my mind pinched me and said, "This is all true, sweetheart!" I smiled feeling relieved.

******

"*Chachu* Sanjay! *Chachu* Ritwik!" My six-year-old nephew Rehaan exclaimed and hugged us as soon as he opened the door. Tugging at my pants he pulled me in to the apartment. "Look what I made at school yesterday *chachu*!" Bringing out a large drawing book, he pointed towards a sketch that looked like a mammal I had never seen before. I'm sure mom would have used that picture to scare us when we were little. Ritwik peering into the book standing behind me exclaimed, "Wow Rehaan! That really is a cool piece of art!" Rehaan beamed while he looked at Ritwik. "Really *chachu*? My teacher gave me 2 out of 10 for this picture though! She said it looked like a cross between a bear and a whale!" "That is exactly what I was thinking!" I screamed out loud. Ritwik glared at me and I looked away sheepishly. Like always, he stepped in to cover up my blooper, "I think your teacher doesn't appreciate a true artist! You obviously can do much better though! You just need a little more practice!" Rehaan was ecstatic; he yanked at Ritwik's hand, pulled him down and pecked him on the cheek. "Thanks *chachu*!" He screamed and ran into his room with his drawing book. All this while, we were oblivious to Mahi and Rajiv standing right behind us, smiling through our animated conversation.

"So how is work with you guys?" Rajiv initiated conversation like any older brother would.

"Can't complain! It is keeping me busy. I just came back from Russia last week; I head to New York next Monday," Ritwik said in response to Rajiv's question. I was now heading Human Resources for South Asia at WSU Life. "Going good, Rajiv!" I dutifully responded.

"You guys wanted to talk to us about something?" Mahi intervened trying to make the conversation a little less clichéd.

Ritwik and I briefly looked at each other and I gave Ritwik the nod to initiate conversation.

"Rajiv, Mahi, we've been thinking. We've actually been thinking for a while now. And looking at Rehaan today just reinforced that decision for us. We want to adopt."

Rajiv and Mahi exchanged a glance before Rajiv spoke, "Look guys, I'm the last person to get in the way of something as noble as that. And I know for a fact that you guys will be fantastic parents. But I'm going to just provide you advice anyway."

"That is exactly what we are here for. Your advice," I said looking in the direction of Rajiv.

"Firstly, how are you going to handle the legalities?" Rajiv probed.

"We've thought about that. We were contemplating Sanjay adopting as a single parent. We know it will be a long drawn process, but at the end of the day it would be worth a shot," Ritwik responded.

"Ritwik, you do realise how tough it is for a single man to adopt, right? Look, the Sandip Soparkar adoption story is a one off case; that definitely does not become a norm. In spite of the guy being famous, rich and reliable, he still had to face a zillion hurdles."

"But Rajiv, if Sanjay adopts through a registered agency, a successful adoption is a possibility. So why not try?"

"And what about work? You guys are both workaholics to the core! How are you going to manage?" Rajiv continued with his questioning.

"Well that is something we'll handle. We've decided that we will take a deliberate call that both of us cannot travel outside the country at the same time. One of us has to be in the city at all times. We'll take turns to come back from work in time. Plus Sunaina said she would provide full support while we're away at work."

"However convinced you guys may sound, I'm not!" Rajiv retaliated, clearly sounding upset by our decision.

Mahi decided to mediate. "Rajiv, when you know these guys would be good parents, why not just let them give it a shot? Plus, there are studies that have proven that the parenting skills of a homosexual couple are far superior to a heterosexual couple. Just the other day, I was reading this article which mentioned that millions of children are being raised in gay households."

"But this isn't the United States of America. This is India," Rajiv was yelling now. He then looked in my direction, "And if you are so keen to be around children, why not work with kids at an NGO or something?"

"Come on Rajiv, that isn't the same! Plus doesn't India offer surrogacy to same sex couples! So what's the big deal around adoption then? There are thousands of kids awaiting adoption anyway? Why not do a good deed and give one of these kids the opportunity to be part of a good home? I don't see a problem. And why are you so dead against it? Are you embarrassed?" I responded angrily.

"No Sanjay! I'm not embarrassed. And I'm hurt that you think that way of me." From Rajiv's tone, it was obvious he was irritated. "I'm concerned about the kid you finally do adopt. Have you thought about what you're going to tell him about your arrangement as two gay men living together? What will you tell him when he asks about not having a mother? What will you do about the constant questioning he will be subject to from his peer group?"

Ritwik and I were taken aback by the constant firing of questions from Rajiv. One look at each other and we knew we didn't have a response to those. We knew Rajiv was making sense. We had of course thought about it while considering adoption, I guess we were being optimistic that nobody else would bring it up. We were only selfishly looking at filling the void in our lives at present. We were really not taking the adopted child's future into deliberation. Why should the child be subject to ridicule and confusion for no fault of his own? How long will he be able to defend us as a couple to a society that thinks nothing of it?

"I hate it when Rajiv is right! Life is so unfair. We would have been good parents," I mentioned to Ritwik on the drive back home.

Looking back, I always had second thoughts about that particular comment I made, 'Was Rajiv really right at the end of the day? Or did we like always just succumb to societal pressure?'

CHAPTER 14

Today I am 46 years old.

I was ecstatic on my way home. Today I unofficially received the information of my appointment as Head Human Resources - Asia Pacific and the Africas at WSU Life. I couldn't wait to share the news with Ritwik. Ironically, Ritwik had news for me that evening too.

In complete celebratory mode, I reached home with a bottle of champagne and a bouquet of flowers. As soon as I entered, I hollered, "Ritwik! I'm home!" I heard no response. Placing the champagne and flowers on the table, walked into the drawing room and saw Ritwik gazing at the busy street while he stood in the balcony. I hugged him from behind and yelled, "I'm so happy today! I'm ecstatic! That is the word I was looking for, ecstatic!" Ritwik slowly turned around with tears in his eyes. He was crying. With a worried expression evident on my face, gently placing the palm of my right hand on his cheek, I enquired, "What happened baby? Everything alright? All went fine in Sydney right?" Ritwik had just returned that morning from a business trip. S&M had just bought out a major soap manufacturer in Australia and New Zealand. Ritwik had to be there to overlook the takeover formalities. Ritwik said nothing in response. He just walked towards the couch and sat down without maintaining any eye contact with me. I screamed nervously, "Ritwik, stop freaking me out! What is wrong?"

He looked towards me slowly and whispered, "I'm sorry baby!"

"Sorry? Sorry about what?" I asked sounding thoroughly confused.

"Please forgive me...."

I began crying out of anxiety, "Ritwik, what is wrong sweetheart? You can tell me, right? Please Ritwik, say something, you're scaring me."

"While I was in Sydney," he began narrating an account whilst staring at the floor, "I was in a book store. I also bought a really good rare book on the history of architecture in Australia for Rehaan. The salesman in fact told me that only 100 copies of that book are available worldwide. At the payment counter, I then bumped into this young 25-year-old guy. We began talking. His name was Paul." A zillion thoughts began running in my head while I listened intently to Ritwik. I was silently praying in my head that the story that was being recounted did not head in the direction I was anticipating. "Paul asked me to come over to his place for a drink. I refused. He begged and pleaded. I obliged. At his place, one thing led to another and the next thing I knew we were having sex. I'm sorry Sanjay. I don't know what I was thinking. I don't even know how it happened. I guess I was smitten because he was so young..." I had stopped listening after I heard the word sex. Ritwik kept speaking; I kept staring in his direction not being able to take in a single word he was saying. I was blinded by images of Ritwik making out with a faceless 25-year-old Australian boy. At the same time, I felt the pain of a gazillion nails being hammered into me. I felt a tear roll down my cheek. I wiped my tear. I didn't want to cry. I felt another tear roll down my cheek. I wiped it again. The tears didn't stop. I screamed at the top of my voice, "You are not going to cry, Sanjay Sanghavi!"

Looking at me hysterically scream out an arbitrary statement, Ritwik hugged me. I pushed him away, "Don't touch me!" I shrieked. With tears endlessly rolling down my cheeks, I questioned loudly, "How could you Ritwik? How could you do this to me?"

"Baby, trust me, I didn't intend to. It just happened. It was an accident."

"An accident? Did you accidentally go to his place? Did you accidentally drop your pants? Did you accidentally have a hard on? Did you accidentally fuck him? Tell me, Ritwik, was this all by accident?" I continued screaming.

Ritwik fell on his knees hugging me at the waist, resting his left cheek on my stomach, "It didn't mean anything to me. It was just futile sex. Please Sanjay, please forgive me. You're way too important to me. I can't live without you. Please don't leave me."

I continued sobbing, "You hurt me Ritwik. You were the last person I thought would ever hurt me. You were like my guardian, you always protected me. I could trust you with my eyes closed. And all it took was a young chap called Paul to break this up?"

Ritwik, hugging me even tighter and wailing even louder yelled, "Please Sanjay, please forgive me. I swear I'll never commit the same blunder again."

I pushed Ritwik's arms away to release his tight grip, "Ritwik, I can't even look at your face right now. Every time I look at you, I picture you having sex with this faceless person. Were you bored of me? Wasn't I good enough anymore?"

"No Sanjay! I told you I was plain stupid! I love you so much; I can never get bored of you." Ritwik was trying hard to convince me.

I walked into the bedroom and shut the door behind me. Ritwik pounded on the door, "Sanjay, let me in. Please, let's talk about this."

"Ritwik, just go away, I don't want to see you or speak to you right now. Please leave me alone!" I screamed.

The next thing I heard was the main door to the apartment being slammed. I spent the entire night crawled up next to the door crying.

******

I was in unfamiliar surroundings. In front of me stood a man with his back towards me butt-naked. "Who is that?" I hollered. The man turned around. I saw a familiar face. "Victor, is that you?" I questioned. Victor began walking towards me. He looked just like the time I had met him in the Philippines. He was young, muscular, good-looking. "Sanjay, you inspire my writing!" he said. He took my hand in his and twirled me around. "Victor, stop it! You're making me dizzy!" I laughed and shrieked at the same time. While I was being twirled, I reached a window pane placed on a brick wall. I wiped the dust off the window and peeped in. I saw a man on top of another man. Tugging Victor's hand, I said excitedly, "Look Victor, two men having sex." The man on top suddenly turned his head in the direction of the window pane. I was scared by the monstrous grin on his face and his blood-coloured eyes. I shrieked. "Ritwik! Is that you?" I asked. I began pounding on the window pane. "Stop it Ritwik! Stop it!" I continued screaming hysterically. The glass wouldn't break. I kept staring while Ritwik continued stroking himself against a faceless man's butt. "I never did sleep with Victor! Love needs to win over lust!" I screamed. I was crying now continuously hammering the window pane with my fists.

I was jolted awake from my nightmare. I had broken into a sweat. My head felt heavy and tired. I looked around to find myself alone in our bedroom lying against the door. Without Ritwik by my side, the bedroom looked empty to me. I knew I had to speak to him. I guess the nightmare I just had triggered an unwanted emptiness. I also realised my relationship with Ritwik was far too important to me for it to end just like that.

I picked up the phone to call him. My call went unanswered once, twice, thrice. Surprisingly, I didn't feel the need to panic. 'He'll call me back.' I thought to myself. I was convinced that my relationship with Ritwik was as important to him as it was to me. And like I rightly assumed, my phone did ring twelve minutes later. But the call wasn't from Ritwik, it was from Rajiv. 'Why is Rajiv calling at this hour? Does he know Ritwik and I had a fight? Maybe Ritwik has gone complaining to him?' Multiple thoughts ran in my head before I answered the call.

"Rajiv, tell Ritwik that he doesn't need to use you as a mediator. He could have just answered my calls," I snapped as soon as I received Rajiv's call.

Not paying attention to a single word I had just said, Rajiv began talking. "Sanjay, I'm picking you up. We need to go to Raman hospital now! Ritwik is serious after an accident. Since I'm listed as one of his emergency contacts, I just got the call from the hospital. Wait for me at the entrance of your apartment building. I'll be there in 10 minutes."

The next thing I knew, I was in Raman hospital fighting back tears while filling a number of forms at the reception desk. Looking at my unsteady hand and tired face, Rajiv pulled the bunch of papers away from me and said, "Sanjay, let me handle this, you go sit with Mahi and Arth."

I didn't have the entire version of what actually happened. Inspector Rao shared with us bits and pieces of what he had heard from witnesses. Ritwik stormed out from home at 1:15 am. The watchman noticed him looking upset. "*Sahab bahut disturb lag rahe the.*" ("Sir looked a little disturbed") were his exact words. He then took the car out and sped out of the building gate at about 1:30 am. Exactly a half hour later, his car was found shattered and toppled over on Avenue Street with him lying unconscious in the driver's seat. It seems he lost control of the speeding vehicle, when he suddenly had to swerve his car to avoid ramming into a drunken man haphazardly crossing the street. The people in the neighbouring slum helped bring Ritwik to the hospital.

I sat next to Mahi dropping my head into my hands. My eyes looked extremely wary from the constant crying and lack of sleep. Shuffling my hair, Arth handed me a cup of coffee and said, "It'll be fine. Relax Sanjay." Taking the cup of coffee from his hand, I looked at him and gently smiled.

It had been an hour since we were all waiting at the lobby area. Every minute of that hour seemed like an hour in itself. I was highly impatient. I remember walking up to the nurse at the reception counter at least 40 times to ask her if she had heard anything from the doctor operating on Ritwik. She was so annoyed by my constant follow up that she finally looked at Rajiv and said, "*Sir, inko sambhaliye, har minute mein status nahin badlega.*" (Sir, please look after him, the status will not change in every minute.) However, my impatience was justified; I had not seen Ritwik since I had arrived at the hospital. Finally, a man in a white coat and green mask stepped out of the operating room and asked aloud, "Who is with Ritwik Kala?"

I walked up to him, "I'm Sanjay. I'm with Ritwik."

"And how are you related?"

Remembering Vikram's experience with Dr Shaikh, I hesitated a bit and said, "We're friends as well as room-mates."

With an extremely cold rehearsed tone, the doctor said, "I'm sorry Mr Sanjay. We were unable to save your friend. He had lost too much blood. We did try our best. You have 20 minutes. We will move him to the morgue then."

And on hearing that, I heard the sobs of Mahi and Arth. But I didn't cry. I just gawked into an empty space. I was completely dazed. All the crying through the night had dried up my tears. But in spite of not crying I did feel the pain. I felt like somebody had ripped my right arm off and was feeding it to stray dogs. I felt like I couldn't move. All the parts of my body suddenly went numb. Rajiv had to literally drag me into the room Ritwik was in.

As soon as I walked in, I noticed Ritwik placed on a bed covered by a sheet with only his head visible. While Arth walked Mahi out of the room since she was frantically crying and was almost out of control, Rajiv stroked his hand on my back and said, "It is ok to cry Sanjay. Just let go. You may feel a little better. I'm stepping out of the room, spend some time with Ritwik."

I heard the sound of a click while the door closed. I continued staring at Ritwik with my head tilted to my left shoulder. I then walked up to him and pulled the sheet that covered him. The doctor had tried his best to clean up the wounds but the large cuts on his chest, stomach and face were still visible. The size of the cuts made it clear that it wasn't a minor accident. It was likely that Ritwik could have died at the spot of the mishap.

I still didn't cry.

I sat next to his lifeless body on the bed he was on and held his hand. It was summer and the air-conditioners were on at full blast. I felt little chills run down my spine. I spontaneously began rubbing my palm against his. I began rubbing it harder. "Are you cold?" I asked him. I got no response. I began rubbing his palm even harder. "You're not dead. You're just cold. Some heat will revive you." Ritwik still didn't move a muscle. Out of my desperation, I began shaking Ritwik's shoulders and quietly instructed, "Ritwik, get up! Who is going to run the business at S&M? They need you." I was distressed by the fact that Ritwik wasn't listening to a word I was saying. I was hysterically shouting now, "Ritwik! Get up! You bloody well not leave me like this! Stop being a fuck'n asshole and just get up! Ritwik! Are you listening to me?" Hearing my shrieks, Rajiv ran into the room.

Rajiv, like always caught hold of me and tried to calm me down. "It was destined to happen. Trust me, Ritwik tried his best to fight destiny, he couldn't." Finally, I felt a tear roll down my cheek. And after that the sobbing just didn't stop.

A few days later, while placing and putting away all of Ritwik's belongings into a box, I came to realise that I was angry and hadn't yet forgiven Ritwik for two reasons - for cheating on me and for leaving me without any closure.

CHAPTER 15

Today I am 55 years old.

"*Chachu*, the apartment plan is all wrong. It is actually a lot more spacious than it looks right now. For starters, we can drop this wall and it'll do wonders for the room." My nephew Rehaan currently based out of Washington DC as an architect was giving me advice on the overall blueprint of my apartment. On his annual visit back home, he had dropped in for lunch at my place. Rehaan had grown up to be a good looking young man. He had a lean body, dressed smartly and had the most contagious smile.

"*Sunaina Mausi kya badhiya aloo ke parathe banaye hain aapne. Man karta hain yehi reh jaoon.*" (Sunaina aunty, you have cooked awesome aloo paratha's. I feel like staying here only). Rehaan complimented Sunaina as she served him food at the lunch table. Sunaina blushed; trying to shift the focus of conversation away from herself back to Rehaan, she said, "*Maine soona tumhari girlfriend bahut gori hain.*" (I heard your girlfriend is very fair). This time Rehaan blushed. I intervened, "*Humaare sahab-zaade ko abhi sirf firangi ladkiyan pasand hain, kya karein?*" (Our man here only likes the foreigners now, what do we do?) We all laughed.

"So how has work been? I hope Washington is treating you well?" I asked Rehaan after Sunaina stepped out of the dining room into the kitchen.

"Work is fantastic! I love it! I'm so glad *Chachu* Ritwik pushed me into this. I vividly remember he was the only one to appreciate my art as a kid. It is so funny how my drawings are making tons of money for my company now." I smiled while Rehaan spoke passionately of his work. "We are however struggling with one project right now." I looked interested in knowing more, Rehaan continued, "There are three companies vying for a single project. This is for an upcoming Zoo in New York. The client kept emphasising on Australian culture, Australian heritage during the brief. I did a lot of research and found out about this book called 'Outback Architecture - The Era Gone By'. Only 100 copies of the book are available globally and I've been trying so hard to get my hands on it. If I get that book, *Chachu* I know we'll get the deal and that would make me a star at work."

A couple of hours later, after lots of banter, Rehaan kissed me on the cheek and said goodbye. As soon as he left I went into my room and stood on a stool to get the boxes I had packed away exactly nine years ago. I never had the courage to open those boxes again. The thought of opening them always led me to mixed feelings. As soon as I tore off the seal from the first box, anger, pain, anxiety, fright all came rushing back to me. I was having an inner conflict with myself on whether I should continue to open the box or not.

I finally decided to open the box.

As soon as I did, I got a whiff of Ritwik's favourite perfume. It really seemed like he was right there. I began running my fingers through his belongings. I picked up the tee he wore to the gym, I picked up the Sheaffer pen he used to write with, I picked up the Tag Heur watch he wore to work every single day. I started to cry. I missed Ritwik but knew for a fact that I had not forgiven him. As soon as I saw the image of Ritwik making out with a faceless 25-year-old, I immediately regretted my decision to open the box. I had been haunted by nightmares with similar images for years now. I tried consoling myself, 'You are only doing this for Rehaan. Find that book Sanjay!'

I desperately started looking through the stuff in the box trying to find the book Ritwik had bought for Rehaan from the bookstore where he met Paul.

"Look at the time Ritwik! It is so late! I'm dying of hunger!

Can we eat now?" I yelled as soon as Ritwik walked through the door. Paying no heed to my yelling, he walked towards me, kissed me on the cheek and smiled. He handed over a Video CD to me and whispered, "This was why I was late." I looked confused. Brushing my hunger aside, curiousity got the best of me and I immediately played the CD. I was taken aback by what I saw. It was the video of an 18-year-old me speaking on the Kashmir issue from the public speaking class that changed my life. With tears in my eyes, I looked towards Ritwik and asked, "Why?" Nearly forgetting that it was the August 15, Ritwik hugged me and said, "Happy Independence Day!"

I continued looking for that book.

"Well, it seems Ritwik Kala has something special to say to a special someone." I was taken by surprise when the presenter on stage suddenly made that announcement. In addition to it being my 38th birthday, it was also karaoke night at one of Mumbai's finest bars Drinks & More. "No way Ritwik, you've got to be kidding!" I laughed while Ritwik walked towards the stage. "Sanjay baby, this is for you!" Ritwik hollered into the microphone. Ritwik didn't even sing in the bathroom, this was obviously going to be a first for him. No wonder he had gulped so many shots of alcohol that evening. He began singing while I smilingly hid my face from the crowd, "Love me tender.... Love me sweet.... Never let me go.... You have made my life complete... And I love you soooooo......" Clearly that was the worst version I had ever heard of the Elvis Presley classic.

'That book! That book! That book! Where the hell was that book?'

"I'm scared!" I hugged Ritwik tightly while we cuddled in bed. "What's wrong sweetheart?" Ritwik asked in response to my random comment. "Gay relationships are so fragile. Do you think we'll be able to sustain ours?" Looking me in the eye, Ritwik said, "We will Sanjay! Without doubt, we will!"

I was suddenly distracted by a set of diaries. The fact that Ritwik sometimes penned down his thoughts in little note books had completely slipped my mind. In spite of my numerous attempts to sneak a peek at his writing, he was always successful in keeping his diaries away from me. I must have overlooked them while packing away his belongings in anger nine years ago.

I read snippets from the diary:

I am adopted. My parents are not my biological parents. I suddenly feel a weird sense of obligation towards them.

I graduated from Wharton today. Mom and dad are so proud of me. Thank god I have been able to meet their expectations.

I'm in the flight back home to India. I hope to find my roots, where I came from. This journey better give me answers to the questions I've been asking for years.

Today I met a handsome young man in an art gallery. His name is Sanjay. As soon as I laid my eyes on him I felt a connection. I was actually courageous enough to approach him and ask him out. He said yes. I'm happy.

I miss Sanjay so much. The distance is getting tougher by the day. There are only 12 months left. I can't wait for the day I'm receiving him from the airport. I promise to never let go of him after that.

The gay life is tough here in India. One of our dearest friends had to go through hell only because he was a homosexual.

I'm the happiest man in the world today. I am legally married to the love of my life in a country called Nepal.

I then deliberately skipped a few pages hoping that Ritwik had mentioned of his trip to Australia and his encounter with Paul. My heart started beating faster as soon as I reached the last few written pages of the diary.

Today I committed the biggest mistake of my life. I met a guy named Paul. Paul was an average looking bloke who invited me over. I didn't want to go to his place; I should have listened to my gut. We were drinking, talking, having fun. He came on to me, I pushed him away. I told him I'm with Sanjay. In spite of that he forced himself upon me and kissed me. The next thing I knew we were having sex. It was strange how I pictured Sanjay's face the whole time. I love him so much. I was extremely drunk at the time, but that is no excuse for what I did. I think I was also smitten because a guy that young was hitting on me. Of course I'm going to let Sanjay know, I'm not in any kind of dilemma about that. Sanjay is my soul mate, my life, he means everything to me. The last thing I want to do is lie in this relationship. I know I made a mistake and I'm praying that Sanjay understands. If he doesn't I will beg, plead, do whatever it takes to make this relationship work. Or else, I will respect his decision and move on. But I'm praying hard, praying harder then I have ever prayed before.

I had tears in my eyes. I began sobbing. I cried even more than the time Ritwik actually passed away. I picked up one of Ritwik's shirts and smelt it. I touched it knowing there was a void in my life. I kept crying. And surprisingly, I felt immense relief. I felt closure. I breathed a sigh and said, "I finally forgive you Ritwik."

The next day, I met Rehaan and handed over the book 'Outback Architecture - The Era Gone By' that Ritwik had bought specifically for him nine years ago. Rehaan was thrilled. He hugged me and yelled, "Thanks *Chachu*!"

I smiled at Rehaan and said, "I need to thank you! Thanks Rehaan!"

******

"Mr Sanghavi, Mr Meeks is here for his 3:00 pm appointment. You have exactly five minutes to wrap up what you're doing now; I'll send him in after that." My secretary Fatima said in an instructive tone. Being the global head of human resources I did not have the leeway to waste a single minute of my time. Fatima was paid to manage my schedule and I had told her when she interviewed for the role that she better do a good job of it or else she will be shown the door. Her instructive tone never surprised me and I do admit that Fatima has helped me manage my desk brilliantly. Till date, I haven't been late for a single meeting except for the times she is away on her annual leave.

"Steve, come on in" I hollered on seeing Steve Meeks at the door to my cabin. Steve Meeks was one of the youngest CEO's in the company. He was 30, held a degree from Harvard, was extremely good-looking and had the body of a fitness instructor. Steve wasn't married and there was always speculation in the office that he was gay.

"Sanjay, I wanted to discuss this new model that is being planned for the country I'm heading. I really think with the right people input, this model can do wonders.

In fact it is so good that it can be replicated across countries. Since this is that big a deal, I didn't want to involve my country HR head. I thought it would be a good idea to get your thoughts right at the inception stage."

"I'm all ears!"

Steve spoke passionately of the new model while I listened intently. At the end of the meeting, I said, "Steve, this model looks good, but I do have some views. It may struggle in certain areas. Leave the presentation with Fatima; I'll have her email my inputs by day end tomorrow."

"Sounds great! I will look forward to hearing from you."

As Steve got up to leave and while I stared at his bubble butt, he suddenly turned around. I quickly shifted my gaze upwards in order to have eye contact with him. "By the way Sanjay, this is out of the professional context, but I would love to take you out to dinner sometime."

"I would love that."

"Great I'll call you."

The very next evening, Steve took me to one of the most expensive restaurants in town. I was obviously anxious before the date since I had not met another man since Ritwik passed away. I wore a casual blazer over a buttoned down shirt and completed my attire with tight fit jeans. Steve looked great in a tight fitted tee, a blazer and low waist jeans. Over dinner, we tried our best not to let conversation digress towards work; we spoke of our travels to exotic locations, Broadway musicals and the ongoing Wimbledon tournament. On the whole, dinner was serene and enjoyable.

"Thanks for dinner! I had a great time." I smiled at Steve before I was to step out of his car to head to my apartment.

Steve gazing into my eyes gently caught hold of my head and kissed me. An image of Ritwik forced me to push Steve away. "What is wrong sweetheart?" Steve asked me. "Sorry nothing, I need to head home, it is getting late and I have an early day tomorrow." "Can't I head upstairs for a cup of coffee?" Steve asked me in the most vulnerable voice.

Steve looked like a ramp model that night. Suddenly, I was distracted. It seemed like his tight fitted tee was calling out to me, 'Rip me off! Rip me off!' it said. His muscular chest and arms were doing a little dance for me. The bulge in his pants seemed larger than the size I would normally fantasize about. It had almost been ten years since I last had sex. Steve, caressing the back of his hand on my cheek, snapped me out of my thoughts. "Well Sanjay, what do you think?"

"Of course, let's go to my place for coffee."

As soon as Steve entered my apartment, I pounced on him like a wild tigress would leap on her bait. Thankfully, Steve didn't push back. That would have been so embarrassing. Steve wanted this too. I came to realise that sex feels as good as it did ten years ago. Of course, the sex ten years ago was notches higher because what I was indulging in right now was emotionless sex.

After we made out while we lay naked next to each other, I slowly touched Steve's lips with my fingers. He suddenly got up to leave.

"Hey, where are you going?" I asked him.

"It is an early day for the both of us, I better head back home," he said while wearing his jeans.

"That sucks!" I said playfully looking disappointed.

"Oh and Sanjay, I forgot to mention. I hope your vote at the next board meeting for the Head of Asia Pacific is for me."

"Come on Steve, let's not talk work."

"Sanjay, of course we're going to talk work now. Your vote as global head of human resources would count twice; this would mean I need to ensure just three more votes for me to get that position."

I was pissed off by Steve's assumption that I would vote for him. "Well Steve, just for your information, Rick is far more experienced, has handled larger countries, has seen more complexities and is definitely a better fit for the job."

Steve responded in an extremely arrogant tone, "Listen

asshole! I don't go around screwing 55-year-old sluts without an agenda. If you don't ensure your vote is for me, I'm going to complain of sexual harassment against you. You won't have the fuck'n guts to show your face to anybody after that. Now you're going to do as you're being told."

And with that statement I was left dumbfounded. I heard the slam of the door while Steve walked out. I couldn't sleep all night. I was in a dilemma of what to do.

The next day after a lot of thought, I did what any principled person would do in a situation like this. I told my boss of the entire incident and tendered my resignation. While my resignation was accepted, Steve Meeks was forced to resign as well.

CHAPTER 16

Today I am 64 years old.

I noticed Dilu and Kelly are graying in spite of their plentiful attempts to coat their hair with product and colour. The wrinkles on their faces too were evident under the single layer of make-up. I caught a glimpse of my receding grey hairline and wrinkles in the reflection on the surface of the mug I was holding. It was obvious we were getting old.

Dilu, Kelly and I were at the local bistro enjoying a cup of coffee, our daily evening ritual. We were like three old women on a park bench while we gossiped.

"Did you know Ayaaz Merchant, that wretched old married man is having an affair with his servant?" Kelly shared the rumour with a twinkle in her eyes.

With our mouths gaping wide open, Dilu countered Kelly, "No way! He is too nice to be cheating on his wife."

"Well, we now know what the definition of 'too nice' for Dilu is." Kelly retorted with a giggle.

After a half hour of frivolous gossip and discussion around hot men which Kelly and I thoroughly enjoyed, Dilu like always interrupted our perky teenage discussion with a thought-provoking question. "So, we're in our 60s now. Any regrets in life?"

I never understood what truth Dilu was seeking by always asking these random questions in between discussions that were not even remotely connected. And it was even more bizarre how we always went into thought when she did ask.

After momentary silence, Kelly said, "I regret being a one man woman. I wish I was like Dheer, a zillion flings even while you're married with no sense of guilt or regret at all."

"Honestly, we still do not know why you're with that bastard? You're way too good for him." I said.

"Sanjay, can you imagine being with another man besides Ritwik even today?" Kelly probed.

Looking away, I softly said, "No!"

"Why? Because you love him right? Even when he is dead you love him. Well, I love Dheer and at least he is still alive," Kelly said sounding upset.

"I'm sorry Kelly; I was just trying to be supportive," I tried calming Kelly down.

"If you want to be supportive, just try liking Dheer," she retorted.

Like always, this time around too Dilu's question led to an unwanted debate. Kelly and I looked irritably at Dilu, like she was the cause of the quarrel, indicating her to intervene to bring this argument to an end. Dilu being her ditzy self took a couple of minutes to comprehend our silent stare and finally said, "Oh! You know what I regret. I regret not having sex with that hot actor I knew from college." "Vir Sahyadri!" Kelly and I unanimously exclaimed. Dilu blushed while she giggled. "Oh that guy was hot! You really should have had sex with him. Plus he was so into you. He could never see anything beyond your breasts," Kelly noisily exclaimed. The waiter at the bistro got worried seeing an old woman of our age scream that loudly, "Ma'am, are you alright? Do you want me to call someone for you?" "No sweetheart we're fine. We were just remembering the good old days." Kelly replied stroking his back.

"What about you Sanjay?" Dilu enquired.

"I don't think I have any regrets. I'm happy with the choices I've made, the life I have led. And every roadblock has been a learning for me," I said casually.

"Really? Don't you regret being true to your sexuality?" Dilu further probed.

"Well obviously there are days where I feel I should

have made the choice of leading a discreet man's life. But is being true to my sexuality my largest regret? Of course not. In fact I do not think that it is a regret at all. "

"But don't gay men usually die alone? That is such a sad feeling. I mean look at how Elvis Presley died," Dilu responded.

Kelly and I looked at each other thoroughly confused. "Elvis wasn't gay, Dilu. I guess you mean the lead singer from that band Queen," Kelly clarified.

"Oh yeah! Freddie Mercury!" Dilu exclaimed.

Overlooking another of Dilu's eccentric moments, I responded with my tone evidently louder, "Dilu, that is such a stupid saga. And truly speaking, have I ever really been alone? I have my family, I have my friends from graduation college, I have my friends from TISS, I have Arth, I have you guys. For Heaven's sake I also have my maid Sunaina and my chauffer Ram. So there, have I really been alone? Why is it necessary for someone to be in a romantic relationship in order to not be alone? Just because I do not have a boyfriend today, I really don't think that makes me a loner."

And this inspiring speech made me realise that there are other relationships in life that need to be given importance. I suddenly felt indebted to the people that I had been with for all these years.

CHAPTER 17

Today I am 75 years old.

The security guard greets me with his usual warm smile, I smile back. The elevator doors open, and as soon as I enter, I notice I had spilled juice on my designer track suit. Upset with myself about how stupid I could be to ruin a track suit that cost me one third of my last drawn monthly salary, I pound on the door of my lavish 2500 square foot apartment instead of ringing the bell. Sunaina, my maid of many years opens the door and with the most sarcastic tone asks, "*Aaj Kya Hua?*" (What happened today?). She looks down at my pants and laughs, "*Arre Sahab, yeh mein do minute mein gaayab kar doongi! Aap ke paas jaadugarni hain, kaay ki chinta?*" (Oh Sahab, I'll get rid of this stain in two minutes! You have a magician with you, no worries!).

I smile at her and move towards the couch. I sit down and switch on the television. The anchor on television is providing reviews on the recently released *The Curious Case of Benjamin Button*. She trashes the movie and I rubbish her review in my head. I smile and think to myself 'What a wonderful movie!'

Suddenly, I feel a shooting pain in my left arm, my chest hurts, I can't see anything.

I just had a heart attack. And while I sit there awaiting death, I look towards the wall in front of me cluttered with self portraits, photographs of loved ones and expensive pieces of art. Unexpectedly, the pain begins to slowly subside and my eyes start to force themselves shut.

A few moments before closing my eyes, I catch a hazy glimpse of the picture of myself posing at the Bangalore Pride Parade and I smile.

******

I opened my eyes slowly. My vision was hazy and unclear. All I could see were the white coloured walls. I could hear a faint beeping sound. I was breathing deeply. I felt all this heavy equipment on me. Looking down at my wrist I saw a bunch of tubes pierced into me. I had an oxygen mask on. I was at the Malabar Hill Hospital.

"Sanjay, how you feeling?" I turned to see Rajiv bending towards me stroking my hair. I smiled.

I looked more closely around the room. It was packed with my close friends and family. Behind Rajiv, stood Mahi and Rehaan. To my left, were Joanna, Rakhi, Saif and Javed. Arth, Dilu and Kelly stood against the door. Next to the window I saw Riya, Kritika and Sonali. I also saw Sunaina fighting back tears and Ram staring at the ground holding the chauffer hat in his hand. Struggling even more with my breathing, I smiled at all of them.

Because of all the heavy medication, I felt like I was suddenly getting into some kind of a trance.

I began envisioning people who were not with me in the room at the time. I saw childhood versions of Sakhi and myself cycling in the park. I saw myself as an eight - year- old tightly holding dad's hand on the giant wheel. I saw mom discreetly handing over chocolates to an overweight teenaged me.

I saw an image of Mr Vaidyanathan smiling at me warmly. I saw a man wearing a skirt continuously twirling. "Sushmita!" I yelled. I saw Vikram and myself dancing the night away in a gay club.

The last image I saw was that of Ritwik. Ritwik was standing looking at me with his infectious smile. He was calling out to me. "Sanjay, we're going to be together again." "I'm coming Ritwik!" I hollered sounding ecstatic.

I gradually opened my eyes again. I signalled Dilu to come close. I struggled to point at the oxygen mask I was wearing. Dilu for the first time in many years knew exactly what I meant. As she pulled off the mask, I whispered into her ear, "Look around, I'm not going to die alone."

And with that, I closed my eyes and passed away. I know for sure that I died with a smile on my face because I honestly wasn't ever alone.

* Section 377; Criminalised sexual activity against the order of nature

On account of Section 377, a doctor is legally bound to inform the police if his patient has contracted HIV through a homosexual act. ~ *Homosexuality and the Indian Physician by Pranab Chatterjee*

There has been an amendment with reference to Section 377 in 2009.

The Delhi High Court struck down the provision of Section 377 which criminalized consensual sexual acts of adults in private, holding that it violated the fundamental right of life and liberty and the right to equality as guaranteed in the Constitution ~ *The Hindu, Friday, July 3, 2009*

Further the Supreme Court declined to pass an interim order to stay the Delhi High Court verdict legalizing gay sex among consenting adults. The court waits for the government to come out with a definite stand on the issue ~ *The Indian Express, Monday, July 20, 2009*

After the amendment, section 377 continues to apply in the case of sex involving minors and coercive sex ~ *Wikipedia*

3756/11/10

Acknowledgements

Rohini. Thank you for listening to me read every single chapter so patiently. The enthusiasm you displayed before every chapter reading motivated me to complete this book. Honestly, this book would not have been complete without you.

Vedika and Shivangi. You'll are like my soul sisters. Being the first people to read, critique and edit Version 1 of the book. I am always indebted to the two of you.

Ajay. You are truly an inspiration and an idol for me. I would not have been where I am at without your contribution and guidance. I love you a lot.

Sunil K Poolani and the team at Leadstart Publishing. Thank you for taking the risk with this book. After multiple rejections from agents and publishers, your courage and support has been impeccable.

Ma, Pa, Nimarta, Meghna, Mary, Sups, Aamir, Owais, Shylu, Sym, Gaurav, Kiran, Vishwanathan Sir, Rohan. You'll have inspired characters in this book. Thank you for just being a part of my life.

The Tata Institute of Social Sciences. I am extremely grateful to every person associated with this wonderful institution. You have immensely contributed to me being the person I am and have provided me the strength to write this book.

Lastly, big thanks to the rest of my friends who I have not been able to mention already. Hashy, Giddy, Pratik, Saher, Shilpi, Amyn, Joey, Ritu, Garima and Rushali. I love you all!